Knife on the Table

Knife on the Table

Jacques Godbout

Translated from the French by Penny Williams
Introduction by Gillian Davies
General Editor: Malcolm Ross

New Canadian Library No. 130

McClelland and Stewart Limited

Copyright © 1965 by Les Editions du Seuil
English Translation Copyright © 1968 by McClelland and Stewart
Introduction © McClelland and Stewart Limited 1976

This book was originally published by
Les Editions du Seuil in 1965
in Paris as Le Couteau sur la Table

0-7710-9230-X

The Canadian Publishers
McClelland and Stewart Limited
25 Hollinger Road, Toronto

Printed and bound in Canada

The characters and events in this novel are fictitious.
Any resemblance they have to people and events
in life is purely coincidental

The translation of this book
was made possible by a grant
from the Canada Council.

**To the Staff of *Liberté*,
as a token of friendship**

CONTENTS

Introduction

It is nearly twenty years since Jacques Godbout published his first collection of poems in 1956. Since that time, he has established himself as one of the most significant and versatile of Quebec artists: he is also a painter, dramatist, film-maker, and founder of the prestigious revue *Liberté*. Although he refuses to confine his talents to any one sphere, it is as a novelist that he has made his most remarkable contribution to Quebec literature, and in particular to what we might term the "novel of revolt". Fiction of the Quiet Revolution of the sixties both reflects and predicts political realities. While a novel such as Jacques Renaud's *Le Cassé* portrays an individual seething with frustrations, and emotionally "broken", the character has no specific focus for his extreme violence. A pre-eminent group of novels—*Ethel et le Terroriste*, 1963, and *Prochain Episode* and *Knife on the Table*, both published in 1965—does have a specific common origin, in the first violent activities of the F.L.Q. The first death to be attributed to them is the point of departure for Jasmin's novel; it is the culmination for Godbout's *Knife on the Table*. In the same way, *D'Amour, P.Q.*, his last novel, reflects some of the events which shook Quebec during the 1970 October crisis. In other ways, Godbout's fiction parallels developments in *québécois* society, in the evolution of the rootless, questing protagonists he portrays. This he does with wit, a painter's eye for detail, and a fine sense of pace. His is an understated art; and while he is less formal and less cerebral than a writer such as Hubert Aquin, he has the same mastery of technique, and is as poetic in his prose. It is this fusion of provocative form and topical content that distinguishes not only *Knife on the Table*, but all Godbout's novels.

Knife on the Table achieves its full significance only when we consider it in connection with Godbout's first novel, *L'Aquarium*. It would be hard to find a more cogent fictional exploration of the state of alienation than in this first book. On the physical level, characters who have come from every corner of the globe are living in the Casa Occidentale somewhere in the tropics. During the rainy season, which coinicdes with the start of the novel, these characters seem to be in the process of decomposition, existing at the level of fish and snails. The narrator and principal character remains anonymous, neither hero nor anti-hero. He is at first an indifferent observer of the other tenants, just as he is indifferent to the revolution which is imminent outside the Casa's walls. He finally escapes his hermetic life, and the reader leaves him on the boat which is symbolic of a new departure, while the other inhabitants of the Casa slowly dissolve in their sodden environment, the metaphoric aquarium.

This aquarium encloses beings who have lost all ideals. The narrator is a character in search of a past with which to identify. He is mired in "la demi-décision", experiencing feelings of impotence and floating. Here, as with the novels of Aquin and Jasmin, one assumes the transposition of problems which are in part nationalist to foreign territory. Sentiments of guilt because of the refusal to accept political responsibilities are basic to the narrator's sense of a failed life; it is a state of mind already made familiar through the works of many *québécois* writers.

Images of rot, of life at a snail's pace, pervade Godbout's novel. His characters are stalked by boredom and coma in much the same way that Aquin speaks of the "catatonie nationale" of the *québécois*. Godbout's men and women are all vertebrates, and yet are explicitly and continually compared first with fish, and then with snails, which are invertebrate, and have, by association, no moral backbone. They no longer fulfil their function as responsible beings; the carnivorous have become slow and fearful herbivores, and thereby assume all the attributes of an inferior species.

The aquarium, for its fish, represents a withdrawal, partly metaphysical and universal, partly nationalist, from life and from moral and political responsibility. If *L'Aquarium* presents us with characters who no longer have any direct contact with the world, in which they *"inexistent"* (to borrow Pierre de Grandpré's expression) then *Knife on the Table* is the logical conclusion to the symbolic departure of the narrator at the end of Godbout's first novel. This time, the protagonist-narrator is a former soldier who has abandoned his army career, but who takes up arms again at the end of the novel, although now it is on his own account (it is his knife which is on the table).

But we should probably start by noting the title, which is overt and incisively bold after the formlessness and dilution implied in the title and content of *L'Aquarium*. Then a similarity strikes us: the anonymity, and consequent lack of identity of the narrator, although *Knife* is narrated throughout in the first person. While Patricia is quite clearly portrayed, there is virtually no physical description of either the protagonist or his second, *québécoise*, lover, Madeleine, for reasons that are closely linked with the theme. The narrative technique, too, resembles that of Godbout's first novel, though here he is even more innovative: in 84 sections there is a free intermingling of French and English, fiction and journalist fact.

The nursery rhyme, "Eenie, meenie, minie, moe," inserted between the title and the first section, states the book's main concern. It implies the necessity for choice: as children, most of us will have used the rhyme to determine who is "out" of a game, and who remains "in". The editors of the French version stress the word "holler", but we might prefer to underline the callous use of the word "nigger", and, if we take it in its generic rather than its ethnic sense, note its relation to Pierre Vallières' *Nègres Blancs d'Amérique*, as well as to all oppressed minorities.

Apart from the narration of events, the sections consist of visual evocations, reminiscence, reflections upon the seasons, apparent *non-sequiturs*, and the frequent use of parentheses for such observations, witty plays on words, and, finally, abrupt changes in tone, ranging from cynicism and caricature to poetic observation. The narrator's imagination moves in all directions. Keeping pace with this movement is the constant movement of tenses from past to present to future, and the constant transition between summer and winter, although the vantage point from which things are recalled or predicted is mainly winter, which has its own thematic importance. The sections also reveal the narrator to us indirectly, in his description of the vaguely sexual movements of the jukebox, for example, or in his statement of his preference for the artificial, like neon, over the natural.

Godbout's narrator, like Gabrielle Roy's Alexandre Chenevert, seems to carry the weight of the world's oppressed on his shoulders. He sees Patricia chiefly as a respite from the burden of these concerns, and also as a link, a "point of organic contact" with the individuals and the world around him, which he fails to experience directly. He and Patricia are "the bohemians of a new race", outsiders and tradition-free, but also free of any responsibility. They both pursue a disordered, hedonistic existence, but the narrator's scorn for the "mediocrity of a papier-mâché life" that Patricia typifies for him is barely concealed.

The whole book, then, is the reflection of a state of mind and conscience, so that the structure, or lack of it, is as digressive and seemingly irrelevant as the narrator's thoughts. Yet characters can be seen as politically symbolic (and in this Patricia resembles Jasmin's Ethel, and Aquin's K); and activity which at first seems haphazard or frankly escapist gives way to activities that are politically or nationalistically oriented. For a long while, the book doesn't seem to have a centre, because the protagonist himself lacks such a centre; he and Patricia, though not personally oppressed or in need, are essentially a rootless and oddly-matched couple, sipping at life in dilettante fashion. For Patricia especially, adherence to popular culture has replaced any religious affiliation: "The local movie-houses are her cathedrals, the bobby-soxers her gods". The narrator feels an increasing bitterness at his nomadic existence, his "incipient gestures, scraps of uneasiness". Patricia is dismissive in face of his existential concerns, and the reader realizes before he does that it is she who is the target for the knife that comes closer to the surface as the novel progresses.

Accidental or deliberate death, and the potential for death implied, for example, by description of the U.S. nuclear arsenal, are reported through factual newspaper clippings. These sometimes appear as footnotes, and sometimes punctuate the narrator's meandering reminiscences, but they are always seen as severed from the purely fictional events of the text, just as they are from the life the narrator leads; they evidently represent the parallel and therefore unreachable world of real life and violent action. It is a means of vicariously enlarging the dimensions of an unfocussed existence: "Are you sure there's nothing for us to do, anywhere, that's important, serious, worth doing?" And the narrator further explores this state in paragraphs in which noise, for example, is described in detail because there is nothing, yet, of consuming interest within the characters themselves. In the same way, the protagonist tells us at length what he and Patricia do, but is evasive about their relationship; his mind is obviously not "anchored"; he darts continually from one topic to another; they compulsively go to movies, seeing the same film four times, walk endlessly, and play charades (as, for example, when Patricia dresses up as a Christmas tree).

He tries to dissipate his anonymity through his lover, "as if for the price of such a mannequin I could buy myself an identity". Patricia is for a while a point of reference amidst his growing restlessness. However, once he is physically satisfied, "Patricia is only a memory". In this restlessness both characters keep returning, actually and in the imagination, to the Lake. It is obviously as significant as the aquarium of Godbout's first novel, an oasis, a verdant place where fantasies can be indulged, a magnet for their imaginations, and an antidote to the monochrome nature of their urban existence. Even the delapidated facades of the buildings give him a "feeling of maternal security". The protagonist's night-mare is that the Lake-bed should dry out, with fish dying in the slime, and that the Lake (it is always called this, even in the original French version) might become fossilized, a part of history, and no longer a symbol of hope.

Mid-way through the novel, the narrator still has not made a decision about what he should do. But decisions are formidable, and it is significant that he wishes to prolong his state of "pre-departure", which has its literal equivalent in the train preparing to leave Vancouver on its trans-continental journey. At the same time, and on another level, the narrator feels the necessity for a personal departure; he wishes to complete the puzzle for which he has only half the clues; and just as there are no distinguishing features to his life, so there is no identity to any of the train stops.

The narrator seems to seek the definition he lacks partly in "pilgrimages" to areas he had lived in as a child; but he soon begins to think less in personal terms, and more in terms of the collective. At the same time Patricia takes a lover, but the protagonist retains his status as a kind of kept man, essentially dependent on her money to keep their affair alive, which echoes the nationalists' view of Quebec as a woman "kept" economically and politically by English Canada. Yet the protagonist conceals his hostility. The knife that he mentions in this connection bears a relevant motto: "mi vida para un amor", which is suggestive of commitment and a secret vocation for sacrifice.

Then the protagonist gets a job, meets Madeleine, and becomes the focus of two women: "I was subject and needed a verb". He discovers that Madeleine is "in my soul", and that Patricia is "nothing more than a land abandoned to the first Englishman who had come along: Madeleine was that conquered country I was slowly, tenderly rediscovering". Patricia grows more politically aware. The narrator continues to feel "at home without being at home. In your skin I am well. In my own I'm uneasy". He has not yet learnt the art revealed in George Lamming's *In the Castle of my Skin*. Although Lamming speaks there of the West Indian negro experience, he is concerned with concepts of identity and worth, and it is interesting to note that Patricia's home is mockingly called the "Castle".

Then Patricia leaves, and Madeleine, who was pregnant, dies violently. She had never been as clearly delineated for us as Patricia had, suggesting what has been implicit throughout the novel, that the narrator and other *québécois* have no identity by which to be known. At the funeral home, the narrator can only think of "desperate cries and nursery rhymes", the latter linking up with the book's recurring emphasis on games, simulation, playing at life. His affair with Madeleine was abortive, and his making love to her sister Monique is fortuitous; both relationships, plus his uneasy one with Patricia, underline the piecemeal nature of his existence. Though assailed by depression, he is able to analyse its cause: "It must be forever circling about a well without plunging into it that upsets me". He finally makes a decision in favour of "the sharp point of awareness". His American odyssey is an attempt at self-annihilation; he travels ceaselessly, always covering his tracks, in the same way he had done, though without realizing it, in Quebec.

Then at last "the games are over"; hostility comes to the surface, and we see the narrator and Patricia as "enemy birds". Throughout the book there are references to the two as birds, sometimes as fighting cocks, sometimes playing at crows, though the breed is not usually specified. They are seen primarily as soft bodies covered with feathers. We can draw some interesting comparisons between these and the fish and snails of *L'Aquarium*. In keeping with Godbout's fish and fowl metaphors in his first two books, we might see *Knife on the Table* as a landmark, in which the characters no longer represent primitive life forms, but the next rung on the evolutionary (or revolutionary) ladder. However, as we have noted, these birds are not birds of prey. They are fledglings in both the literal and figurative sense, and as such are still vulnerable. The bird images take on their true significance when it becomes clear that through the act of choosing, of commitment, the "aviary" may be destroyed. The news clipping of an F.L.Q. bombing at the end of the novel testifies, for the narrator, to the fact that the overt political struggle has begun in earnest. In such a flight to freedom or political fulfilment, discovery of an identity perhaps, wings may be broken, but such a flight is imperative because "hatred has come like a season", and we are familiar with the seasonal migrations of birds in search of more propitious (in this case political) climates.

Patricia symbolises, for the objectives of the novel, the Anglo-Saxon world, although she has a Czech father and an Irish mother. For her lover she is "a bit of that tinsel, that world of parvenus, that chrome that speaks English". Other critics have pointed out the bitter-sweet nature of the relationship between them, in that Patricia is both loved and resented. Once Madeleine is dead, the affair deteriorates to the point at which the underlying hostility becomes open antagonism. The liaison can be seen as a metaphor for the gradual evolution of a political conscience and a sense of identity, which replaces the allegiance of the lover. The feeling of malaise increases to the point of revolt, and the final act of affirmation: the unsheathed knife, signifying division and violence, will remain "on the table" as a symbol of imminent revolutionary acts.

Salut Galarneau! renews the examination of similar problems in its main character, François Galarneau. In this third novel, Godbout gives his protagonist not only a name, but the faculty of self-analysis. He is a hot-dog seller with a unique method of exorcising his frustrations: "When I grill my hot-dogs, I dream that they're priests sizzling at the stake. I make my revolutions in the grease drain of my stove". When he utters the title phrase "Hail, Galarneau!" he is rejecting his alienation, and affirming his reintegration into society. Here Godbout presents us once again with a nationalist theme, but this time in the guise of a quest for identity and self-mastery on the individual and moral level.

The ambiguous title of Godbout's last novel, *D'Amour, P.Q.*, refers to one of the principal characters as well as to the province of Quebec. This fourth book also has a political significance and may be seen as a "dialogue intérieur" on Godbout's part, in which he considers the relationship between the alienated writer and society. The novel Thomas is writing describes events which take place in Africa. It is with his secretary Mireille's help that he rejects his preoccupation with words and fictional intrigue and gets to the heart of real and more immediate problems.

In a sense, Godbout himself has followed a similar literary path. Whereas *l'Aquarium* is set in a tropical country, probably Africa, *Knife on the Table* takes place on home ground, and demonstrates an attempt at "désaliénation" on the part of the protagonist. (Could it be the same anonymous character in both novels, in that one's experience completes the other's?) Galarneau relives the process of alienation — revolt — disalienation; and the same process begins again in *D'Amour, P.Q.*, a novel in which the conclusion translates a new hope, definitive this time, it would seem. "Servilité terminée!" says Mireille. It's an exclamation of independence in the mouth of the least orthodox of all Godbout's characters; and with her statement she evokes not only an individual sense of liberty, but the collective one which Godbout's other novels sought through diverse symbols and metaphors.

Of all the contemporary novelists of revolt, Godbout's works are the least pervaded with violence. All his novels involve revolutionary acts or attitudes, but physical violence remains latent rather than actual. Apathy and violence are opposing symptoms of the fragmentation experienced by the alienated individual. Godbout seems dubious about the efficacy of violence as a reaction to alienation, whether the violence be verbal or physical. He and other *québécois* writers concerned with the search for identity suggest that alienation is a state of mind that can best be dissipated through commitment of either a literary or a revolutionary kind. Literary analysis of such a state of mind is in itself the equivalent of the kind of awareness that must precede any revolutionary transformation. This is why we might "Hail Godbout!" as one of the first novelists to achieve the ré-appropriation du monde et d'une culture" of which he speaks in his preface to the French version of *Knife on the Table*.

Gillian Davies
St. Thomas University

AUTHOR'S NOTE

This book is, above all, the story of a rupture. A rupture between two human beings who love each other but who at the same time have become victims of a *situation*, in the Sartrian sense of the word. Also: Today there are things, events, facts that a French Canadian no longer wishes to explain. (It's not weariness, but when you spend all your time explaining, someone else does all the living.)

Of course, this book is still part of French literature, but it is perhaps closer to the literature of *francité*, as defined by Jacques Berque, the well-known sociologist and specialist in Algerian affairs, who was the first to describe the only *commonwealth* people in Dakar, Brussels, Paris, Lausanne, or Montreal do possess: a common language, thus a common *structure*. And from now on, writers *outside* France, using the French language as a medium of communication, cannot play the "Paris game" anymore: a game that permitted the Metropolis to define taste, style, story line, etc.

This novel is not a French novel about Canadians but a Canadian novel written in French. This is probably why critics in Canada and France wrote that the French edition of *Knife on the Table* marked another rupture too: the end of a "French literature in America," the beginning of an American literature in French.

TRANSLATOR'S NOTE

Throughout the French edition of this book,
many words, phrases, and even
entire sentences appeared in English.
These have been set *in italics*
in the English translation.

1

Eenie, meenie, minie, moe,

Catch a nigger by the toe,

If he hollers let him go,

Eenie, meenie, minie, moe.

1

"I received a letter from *mother dear*."

". . . ."

"She's in Florida. Toasting herself in the Miami sunshine."

"With some other widows?"

"Of course. Laura Stanson is with her, Mary Dew and old Jane Barnhill."

"All four out on a spree!"

"They're talking about buying a house and never coming back to this insane climate."

"And your father worked himself to death for that?"

"No, you idiot! *Because my father left a few million dollars behind him*, you want my mother to distribute it all to little orphans?"

"That's how rich people usually assuage their good consciences. It's even the thing to do."

"Honey, you really do disgust me sometimes – especially when you talk money. While we're on the subject, how are your creditors?"

Sullen, I break off the conversation.

"They're very well, thank you, and so is the head of the morality squad. They cheese me off."

[Meeting Patricia that summer didn't create it, but it certainly widened the cleavage between myself and those with money. And anyway, I was so poorly paid in that army of idiots that at the end of September, when I finally decided never to set foot in camp again, I left my uniform and cap behind with great satisfaction. I looked upon myself as both deserting and disinterested – which pleased both my Tarzan-like taste for adventure and my political instincts. Salary and pension, up the Colonels! Today I don't give a damn about the army, right side up or sideways.[1]]

[1] New York (AFP) – The August 23 issue of *Time* magazine, now on sale, carries an article about the

2

A shaft of light filtering through the shutters alights on the bed sheets. Patricia spreads her legs. She says she would like to be penetrated by the winter sunshine. . . .

atomic arsenal of the United States, the most powerful nation in the history of the world.

"This arsenal," writes *Time*, "now includes: 125 Atlas intercontinental missiles, each with a 5-megaton atomic warhead (one megaton equals the explosive force of 1,000,000 tons of TNT); 68 Titan intercontinental missiles, with 10-megaton atomic warheads; 150 new Minutemen missiles, two-thirds of them installed within the last six months and 800 more coming in the next two years. These missiles have atomic warheads of 800 kilotons; 144 Polaris missiles with 800-kiloton warheads installed on 9 submarines (32 more submarines and 512 missiles will be in service in 1968); 400 Hound-Dog air-to-ground missiles armed with 1-megaton bombs.

"Apart from these weapons," adds *Time*, "the Air Force has 2,000 bombs of 10 megatons carried by 720 old B-47 bombers and 80 new supersonic B-58s."

And 24-megaton bombs are carried by the B-52s of the Strategic Air Command.

"Such a bomb," writes the weekly, "dropped over a large city, would burst into a ball of flame about 4 miles in diameter, triggering flash-fires for 40 miles around, digging a crater one mile wide and several hundred feet deep. It would release a gigantic cloud of poisonous radioactive dust that would climb 25 miles in the air; the fall-out could kill people 350 miles from the site of the explosion. The United States has more than 1,600 bombs of this strength on 630 B-52s, ready to be fired. With this nuclear arsenal, the United States is the most powerful nation in the history of the world."

2

Outside, the sunshine bursts like a blown-up bag, punctured as if by a trumpet blast. People look at each other through lowered eyelashes; the white is so intense it seems to possess its own light. Yet the air scarcely moves enough to transmit sound. And everywhere the piled-up snow, like linen to be washed.

[My only memories of similar suns are memories of sleeping in dust and dryness (and the vultures beating their wings); somewhere else.]

Or again: That tablecloth of water where the reflected light, like stones skipping off the waves, forced our eyes to hide behind narrowed lashes, forced me to turn aside as if from a horrible sight.

3

A red dress kicked to the bottom of the bed. Red suits her so well that I often felt cuckolded in the streets by the attentive glances she drew. (That was in 1952.)

(In the shower, Patricia takes pleasure in lathering the soap around her breasts. Patricia always stays too long in the shower, as if she were forever rediscovering her virginity or her complexion. In vain I tell her every day that the plaster behind the yellowing ceramic tiles will fall if it gets wet, will crumble away like bad make-up, that she must curve her shoulders and her back so the drops won't fly about, so the splashing water will flow, will lick the body. . . .)

4

Far off, behind the farthest houses, on Baker Street, you reach the solitary Hillock where people go to see the horizon circle the ground with a blue line of air, like a precise scar.

Every noon we go there with the others, who arrive in little groups, as if for a strange Mass where each awaits his own special god who never comes.

"Bonjour, Matthew."

"*Hello.*"

"*Anything new?*"

"*Jesus saves!*"

"How's old Edith?"

"*Dead. It's very sad.*"

"You can't spend your life being born."

"*Hello Patty!*"

"*Good day, Mr. Black.*"

"Look at the airplane over there."

"It's a bird, dear, you're worrying for nothing."

"*Let us sing, brothers, let us pray.*"

In the upper room
In the upper room
With Jesus. . . .

You must build towers and pyramids on these plains, navel of the continent, so that – from their summits – you can better measure the emptiness, the immensity that envelops the snow, and then the wheat which surrounds us in the summertime, to the west. . . .

In the winter, there are no odours.

Yet it was harvest-time. Not that either of us took part the way city people do (straw in the hair, ridiculous clothes, playing the Sunday peasant), but that month we both had lazy weekends to fill. All August the shortened English week: I left camp Thursday evening and returned Monday morning; she did the same since she was enrolled in summer courses at the local university. I played at soldier, she at the intellectual: we should have been framed and exhibited in a display of the International Middle Class. . . .

"I enjoy the shower so much that I'd make love *tout seulement* to have another one. . . ."

"*Tout simplement!*"

". . . *tout simplement* to have another one. Thanks."

"It's ridiculous how you're forgetting your French."

"Oh."

"Do you remember: the accent I insisted on, the endless corrections of structure?"

She smiled with all her freckles, studied her arms with nonchalance.

She takes a wicked pleasure in walking about nude, laughing throughout the room while, propped up with a pillow at the head of the bed, I follow her with my eyes, an avowed caress; her white back striped by the light from the Venetian blind, a zebra body, then the black, the shadow of the wall when she leans, then one shoulder in the light. . . . (What was that story Père Genest, the Jesuit Professor of Morality, used to tell us about a tribe whose sense of decency insisted they walk about nude . . . with their shoulders covered? I remember he shook with pleasure.)

5

There's something artificial about oases, a coagulated appeal, controlled colour, order in the type and the number of the trees. This oasis had all the refinements: a lake dug by government bulldozers, geometrically surrounded by green and blue conifers and cabins built of round varnished logs (*rustic log cabins are so sweet*), marked here and there with lettered signs of imitation birch-bark, set off with immense camping grounds that supplied everything, running water to wash the dishes, wood cut and dried in advance, cement pits for camp fires (*be careful, help prevent disasters*) . . . only use and time, helped out by huge invitations to drink Coca-Cola, Pepsi-Cola, and Orange Crush, and by the green neon of the motels (*vacancy*) have managed to transform the Lake into an habitable place.

But the Lake was the only spot within three days' driving that offered a little shade and fresh air. It had two bowling alleys and the only dance hall in the area. And the only stable. Patricia went there for the horses (*horse chestnut or chestnut horse?*).

At noon the sun and the wind allowed us to amuse ourselves with imaginary mountains, to conjure up mirages. At midnight we entrenched ourselves in the amusements room, where we tried to rediscover those myths about the West to be won. (Playland-*vérité*: In one corner, a life-sized machine clothed in black and disguised as a disreputable cowboy that offered to test one's shooting skill for ten cents. The girls were particularly fond of it. And a record spat out insults for every missed shot, just to add to their pleasure.) As well, behind the painted windows, there were safaris, wars, aircraft carriers. . . .

"*Would you throw my shoes this way? Please?*"

Patricia puts on her dress with the delicate care of a flower filmed in slow motion, and transforms herself into a spot of blood against the wall, into salvia like those in the beds of the quartermaster's barracks. (*Baraquer:* to crouch, with reference to the camel.) The Camel that summer was a Colonel brought from London to teach us how to march in rows and to recite lessons in military law.

He would appear on ceremonial and parade days, smooth-shaven, scrubbed, polished, ironed like an altar-cloth of the Grey nuns. He put on a show of stringless marionettes, and we had the anonymous role of the chorus. His wife, a big Englishwoman with over-long feet, each of which went its own way, sat stiffly erect on a light wooden chair. She held us trapped in her gaze, and her eyes never dropped. The Colonel reached orgasm by making us run on the spot. For sure, she chose that moment to pick the huskiest men for the soirée, inviting them to come for tea, and trying them out one after the other. The wife of a Colonel, whose backside must have been like two slices of lemon. *Iced tea.*

"Why did you come back?"

"I don't know yet. For you. For the security of your money, perhaps, for your health."

"Really?"

"I don't know: All America seemed to me as empty as the palm of my hand."

"Out of complicity?"

"If you like . . . complicity, prestige. . . ."

That reassures her. We walk side by side, we support each other, for the ice under the snow defies balance at every step. Outdoors, in her fur coat, Patricia is nothing but a happy face meeting the cold. Her skin tightens in the wind, firms itself, it's a return to childhood with red cheeks, wool scarves over her mouth, chapped lips, eyes weeping deliciously.

Soon a weird tint of blue will begin to stain the snow banks, then, as the houses become less frequent, the snow will harden, and the mounds will grow taller in the fields.

———

6

I lay on the beach of the artificial Lake trying to get a tan or, when the sun hid behind the trees, I tried to interest myself in the comings and goings of the children with their buckets, their shovels, their balloons of coloured polyethylene, in the slow cortège of old ladies with work-ravaged legs and thighs striated with varicose veins. They seemed to be the decrepit columns of a vanished kingdom. I wasn't bored, I was recuperating; not being a very good athlete, I had simply worn myself out in those stupid training courses where we had to carry on our backs all the furnishing for a machine-gun nest, stumbling among the wild raspberries while the Colonel drove along the paths, sitting in his jeep like Caesar in an illustrated dictionary. I wasn't bored, I was perhaps dead tired; and also all the young girls wore white metal bands to keep their teeth in line, which sometimes gave them, despite their thirteen years, the ridiculous appearance of a tomboy who refuses to grow up; also, young women weren't numerous, and the very rare ones who did live at the camp came down to the Lake with their husbands. Only the Swedish women who had come to study the latest inventions of American aviation could have, on certain Sundays, provided us with entertainment. . . .

"Why come back here then?"

"I love you. It's simple. And then, I have a short memory: you help me to live twice. If I say: 'John Jarrel,' you help me trace his appearance, remember the colour of the horrible ties he wore Saturday nights, describe the smell of the boutique he had on Summit Circle, you remember the red Buick convertible he had. . . ."

"I think it was blue."

"You see? And this shade of mauve in the street when he came to pick us up near the Spanish restaurant, one Thursday night."

"You didn't came back just for that?"

"No. Of course not."

We have been walking so long that the snow fades in the light, and the whitening sun seems to cool down for the end of the world. Now the road is hardly any greyer than the horizon where already the eye can see nothing.

Everything is so clean . . . so monstrously *English*, my friends would say, if they could see these streets gleaming like the bottom of a bathtub, scrubbed with Ajax, surely.

We've crossed the western district without finding a single thing lying around. (Not even an abandoned garbage pail, which could have been left half-buried in the snow.) The only available distraction is to count the Presbyterians leaving their chapel of white wood, perhaps happier to be together again than to pray.

Mustn't be left alone, facing the snow.

But the pastor is complaining that fewer and fewer people are coming to sing the praises of the Creator and that he can hardly get a decent foursome together for the Wednesday evening service: television antennas scattered in the heavens, fastened to the chimneys to prevent wind damage, offering their prayer to the world of entertainment. Coming back along the main street, for many years the only street in town, we count the antennas thrusting their steel corsets into the diffused light, like a cloud of petrified insects on the city's roofs.

(It's still incredible that we can concentrate on this emptiness above ourselves and not pick out the words and sounds gathered by the antennas.) And I know by heart the songs which the crooners must be murmuring on the local Hit Parade, on Channel Nine, at this very minute:

I'm in the mood for love,
"*. . . .*"

Patricia. The same songs played for us by the juke box which, for ten cents, lit up so prettily, strutting like a peacock, swelling with the colours of the rainbow from top to bottom the length of its neon tubes. With gentle trembling motions, like a sexual gasp, the mechanical arm chose one of the thirty-five records (B-12, C-21, D-30, a quarter) set in rows like books in a library.

(At the same moment, the male half of the room hurried to the other half, which a sign hung from the ceiling by two copper chains pompously called *Ladies*, jostling each other to get there first.)

Usually I let several dances go by, taking great care to pick out, from the magma of infatuated teenagers and old hens, the one girl who was worth my time, worth talking to, holding against my body as I followed the pulsing rhythm blaring from three loud-speakers strategically hidden in the greyish ceiling.

From time to time a policeman checked the room for alcohol, slightly ridiculous in his old-fashioned riding breeches and his Mounties hat; each time the bottles slid under the tables and resurfaced once he had passed the door. And since his inspections took place on schedule, we knew (he knew) that he would never catch anyone by surprise. *Save the surface, you save all*, my father would say about the Irish, then he would spit on the ground; I did the same.

7

In front of the office of the *Free Press*, under a wirephoto reproduction in stark blacks and whites, and even more dramatic because of it, a photograph showing an Uncle Tom in glasses in the left-hand corner who seems to be doing a little dance to avoid two white cowboys: "Mounted police make a Negro grimace with pain by poking him on the back with electric cattle prods."

(Reuters.) — Last night police arrested 104 Negroes taking part in a peaceful demonstration against racial segregation in Plaquemine, Louisiana. 85 demonstrators, 33 of them children, had been arrested during a previous demonstration of the same nature. They were charged with disorderly conduct in a public place.

Meanwhile, in Chicago, Rev. Martin Luther King predicted other racial incidents in Birmingham. Referring to the recent bombing incidents, King said: "This city could soon be the scene of a night of violence."

[Not so long ago, these incidents would have seemed impossible to us, or only possible at the other end of the world, or we wouldn't even have known anything about them; now if they torture members of the Socialist Party, the *Union nationale des forces populaires*, in Agadir, it's as if it happened just two streets over. (Universal man is born and we don't realize it.) But Patricia refuses to read the papers or listen to the news on the radio and television: am I in love with her calm ignorance? It bothers me. Stupidity. Yet one must make realities coincide.]

8

The warmth of Patricia's breath made a clear spot on the frosted window of the biggest jewelry shop in town. We peek through it one after the other, looking for some distinctive ring to come back and buy tomorrow. (Patricia has a collection of rings, and for her pleasure we got engaged six times that summer.) "A silver band, a blue Cabochon stone." She winks, we have chosen.

Is it her high forehead that gives her that look, or is it the steel of her eyes?

(*Mother, what is love at first sight?*)

(Oh, no, my son, such dramatics: the sin of pride – once you understand, you want to go on and know more and more. . . .)

Now the cold magnifies tenfold the strident call of the sirens in the streets of the lower city and the indecent scream of jet engines, which could easily throw us against rough cement walls tossed up like the tufts of a carpet; air in this temperature is a crystal which vibrates dangerously under the unforseeable oscillations of high frequencies. The cry of a child reverberates through the city turned echo chamber.

"You know the little Chinese who are dying of. . . ."[1]

[1] Here you don't choose the restaurant for its cuisine – they're equally antiseptic and identical whatever

12

9

The artificiality of the Lake was as endearing as a spaniel: those façades especially. All of them were ready to be torn down, but they gave me more of a feeling of maternal security than I would have had living among stones thousands of years old, or with my feet in fountains dominated by antique statues. [Patricia is a bit of that tinsel, that world of parvenus, that chrome that speaks English. Synthetic. It's a whole race of Americans – and of English Canadians – who think an automobile museum as important as the Parthenon. Perhaps more (some summers they go off fifty or sixty strong in old Fords and travel the country, for nothing, to show people – what do you know – they've kept intact something going back to 1920). Completely nuts. The world of business? I like it the way I like neon. The way I prefer those terrible television series to a serious concert. The way I am partial to fires everywhere that make us forget the night, décors that shout at you, lights so vivid they kill the sun, publicity. . . .

[Patricia is my weakness, my bog, my point of organic contact with those 190 million individuals that surround me. My little catechism of multi-coloured emptiness. And after all, you can't be forever preoccupied with Negroes, the Cold War, and the little Chinese

the dish – but rather for the roughness of the décor, or even for its name: in mid-winter, when your earlobes whiten with cold, there's a certain pleasure in eating at the Monaco Café even if you eat bad food. The desired exoticism not being any more disillusioning than the accidental exoticism of certain realities. On the contrary. Anticipating our surprise and limiting our desires, the green plastic ferns and philodendrons finally give off their own contagious perfume.

who die of hunger while you're swallowing fried oysters and cockles in white wine.]

(A body, a beautiful body, Patricia, not a single line in your face, and not boyish and stupid: she was so young when we met that she had to dress up if we wanted to go to movies restricted to those eighteen and over. But she has matured and learned: today she can discuss love and death, her knife pointing toward the heavens, without a nervous gesture, her fork ready.)

"Doesn't it get you down, darling, to carry the entire world like that on your shoulders? *I mean, come on, get that chip off your shoulder!* I'm not a racist, but the only Negroes I've known have been porters on the train. *I can't get upset like you.* . . . Does it really kill your appetite?

10

Young girls, who came to squander a few days of their vacation at the oasis, usually arrived two by two: one pretty, the other a real dog. Patricia was alone, and alone at a table in the Paradise Dance Hall. She didn't seem either bored or pleased. She refused to dance, but she told me she would be glad to go to the restaurant with me even if she had already eaten. . . . Patricia eats a lot, with gusto, and never gets fat. From then on she cost me, every weekend, my entire pay for the week. I almost had to go without beer and cigarettes at camp so I could pay for the weekend festival. And that was when I began to sell shell cases on the black market – to merchants for the copper, and to veterans for the memories.

"How long did you stay in Tampico?"

"It wasn't Tampico. It was much farther down. Three years. Some months. Why?"

"I'm figuring, that's all."

She and I were then really the bohemians of a
new race: gypsies without a past, mediocre, without
traditions, without a virgin at the ocean in the fall,
without rosaries, without horses to feed (and yet how
Patricia likes pressing her thighs around the sweaty
body of a pureblood too old for the Queen's Plate, but
still lively enough for a holiday trot!).

Happy to brush my finger-tip against the mediocrity of a papier-mâché life (as if she went her way
through prefabricated décors, and we were seated in
one of those little electric trains that children ride in the
big stores during the Christmas holidays: Bambi,
Jumbo, Mickey, Superboy, the mythology of Walt Dis-
ney was more familiar to us than that of the elves and
the will-o'-the-wisps). Patricia believed in excessive
noise or exaggerated silence. Sometimes she made me
dance six records in a row, sometimes she took me by
the hand in the middle of the night, down to the sand,
which we knew would be cool on the surface and then
warm once our fingers dug in.

We would stay there, facing the wall of shadows
thrown by the cedars. We were listening, I think, to
crickets, to our hearts; we weren't yet twenty.

(*Let's go man, let's.*) But I didn't want to sleep.
[I have always been afraid of sleep (though I sleep a
lot), afraid I might not wake up. At the Lake, at the end
of a night, on King Street, my biggest put-down was the
successive closing of the boutiques, the playlands, the
restaurants which refused to serve a last sandwich, a
last cup of coffee.]

11

It was a strange love, almost one-way: I dreamed
of her all week, but because we were of different lan-
guages and cultures, I had trouble imagining her days,

her thoughts, her childhood. I wore myself out for her, I polished my brass, I waited. I was Waiting itself. I was indifferent to the others, and they returned the compliment. In camp men can only avoid total brutalization with their nerve-endings. When night came and the sun was endlessly setting, unable to dream on their beds because the rooms were as dreary as college dormitories, they would gather at seven o'clock around a fire, a few cases of beer, and rye whisky.

I remember whole evenings spent in semi-sleep contemplating the black wood of the piano – the only surface where graffiti could be gouged – scarred from chairs, pen-knives, use. The rest of the furniture, the chairs, the tables, was replaced almost monthly, after a donnybrook, just for the hell of it, or a mass battle between two sections carrying on the old French-English quarrel. Wearing the same uniforms, obeying the same orders, the soldiers in khaki green mixed it up. French Canadians used their boots to avenge the deportation of the Acadians, the loss of Louisiana, the sacrifice at Dieppe; the English defended their rights over America and the little colony of Quebec.

The next morning the Camel, who could sense our quarrels but didn't understand them, would make us jump, run, and threatened us with barrack inspection: most slept that night beside their beds, on the carpet, so as to keep the covers smooth and the neat hospital corners.

The English caroused awkwardly and stupidly but, sunk in a leatherette chair, eyes half-shut, I soaked up a whole military folklore which used to make Patricia laugh. The songs were probably bawdier than I realized (they taught me English with a Prairie accent), and the puns often escaped me.

> *Old King Cole*
> *Was a merry old soul. . . .*

"Are you cold?"
"Not at all."
"You came back despite –"

16

Despite the cold, despite the creditors, despite the fear, despite hatred, despite a whole love to begin again, seize again, renew. Patricia, the first Patricia, the second as in the days of royalty, I came back for several days, for two hundred years perhaps.

12

A Salvation Army officer stands at the door of the cinema, holding out a leaflet. I sense there'll be a sermon on the pillow in our room tonight: nude, letting me caress her freckled white body, she'll prove to me the existence of a God she's invented during the movie, just to make me sweat, because she knows that I don't believe. In the same way (*I like to tease you*), what made me miserable at the Lake was the single shabby movie theatre that played one movie all week: During one rainy weekend Patricia, her head on my shoulder, made me sit through the life of *Houdini le Magicien* four times (not because she liked it so much, but because she was fascinated by the narcissicism of making a film, itself the art of illusion, about an illusionist). And after watching the same episodes four times in colour, I believed in them more and more – perhaps out of sheer fatigue (the candies you crunch in the dark, a B-film, lovers nuzzling each other at the back, old people asleep, chewing gum stuck under the seats, all are indispensable)....

The local movie houses are her cathedrals, the bobby-soxers her gods. One must bend to the rites, to the ostensible signs of the cross, dipping one's fingers in the holy-water basin of hot popcorn in salted butter.

"Do you think love can begin again?"

"*I can't listen to you and Bogart at the same time!*"

A moment ago we came back along the main street; in the icy night the twenty-four-hour drugstores make squares of light in the grimy snow, the grey rectangles of other geometric figures as well, which transform themselves as you approach them, trample them, cross over them; a game.

And then, winter nights would be sad to the point of tears without that flashing brightness like bursting noise which forces passers-by to lower their eyes, perhaps because of the dazzling light, perhaps also because of swirls of wind-driven snow which begin to fall, first sifting down like the last daisies of July, then with greater and greater intensity, stranger and stranger, killing the noises one by one, even heaven itself, offering sleep in a night without birds.

$\dfrac{2}{3}$

14

"What is the matter?"

"I'm at a turning point of my life. . . ."

"Every day is a turning point!"

"But I feel that, this time, it's going to be a very sharp turn. Maybe it's not even a turn, perhaps I'm at the end of the road and behind the wall, there's nothing, a cul-de-sac. . . ."

I say it without believing it. You know that as well as I do. Why die? We were born to a silver spoon and an engraved cup. What have we been doing since? Moving in and out of tenderness, giving ourselves and taking ourselves back. I've played the game a long time, and I've played it poorly.

What kills me is that I don't know anymore what's at the end of the trip, or what station . . . I've come full circle: we left from here, here I find you again. Hello Patricia.

"And now what?"

15

The first weekend, content with passionate gestures, we never made love. I wondered about the consequences of that act which – according to boys in the street – is so simple; yet so difficult when you tremble with tenderness and desire. Patricia actually led me under the band-shell in the middle of the park; we pressed against each other in silence behind the ornamental latticework of its walls, clutching and releasing without truly embracing each other, breathing and then smothering our breath in a kiss longer and more lingering than in the cinema, reassured by the sighing presence of other couples in the dark (probably as foolish as we were). But those hours we spent rolling about in the dust satisfied neither our senses nor the strange attraction that we had for each other.

(Even today I cannot explain the need I had for a woman who was a total stranger to me. And in those days I liked to kiss the tip of her breast and repeat mechanically, "Nordic skin;" then let my lips wander over her face, "northern eyes, the hair of a Nordic blonde, a northern tongue," as if for the price of such a mannequin I could buy myself an identity.)

Several weeks later, Patricia made me rent a room in one of the most luxurious hotels at the Lake. Everything there was imitation but well-done imitation, false good taste by the square yard. Wall-to-wall cocoa-brown carpets. Walnut veneer finish on the bed. White perforated acoustic tiles in the ceiling. A bathroom that could have handled a family of twelve on Saturday nights. And then everywhere, over lamps or beside dressers: Dufy or his brother. Quality reproduction, a Simmons air-circulation mattress; lattice windows looking over the Lake. The song of brown owls and the cry of screech owls. . . . I never knew if they were real or if the night also had its own artificial life (one could imagine an enterprising company putting loud-speakers here and there, and playing records of crickets and bats all night long) —

Sounds to dream by.

16

Patricia has left me alone. I scribble notes on a yellow paper-napkin. In the margin I draw flowers, rockets, suns, patience. Patricia has left me alone. And without even a newspaper. The room is wan. How many years before the police forget about a dossier? Five, perhaps. . . .

This morning we went down to the airplane field. And as we walked we breathed through tightened, half-closed nostrils an icy, secret air which prickled our lungs. Seen upon arrival, from the top of the skies, the city looks like a game of coloured blocks left by a distracted but orderly child in the snow. But right next to the airport, the effect is almost identical to walking through the streets: miniscule buildings, like abandoned trap-shooting cabins, sleeping, protected by enormous layers of snow thrown up by the snow-blowers after every storm. We were talking about truth, I think, but Patricia cut short the discussion by leading me to the control tower where three technicians she knew were directing the indolent comings and goings of the jets.

"Charlie" (said Patricia, gesturing like a vaudeville act) "is the good lord, you know; from the heights of his electronic cloud he directs the interstellar traffic." (Charlie laughed, saying, *Goddam, why don't you speak English, Patricia.*) "He says one word and he spares lives, all he has to do is be silent and a hundred people are wiped out."

(UPI) A Caravelle transport belonging to Swissair exploded in flight near Zurich this morning, carrying to their deaths the eighty people who were aboard. Police have confirmed that there were no survivors.

The plane, which had just left Zurich for Rome, crashed near the village of Duerrenanesh, some twenty kilometres from the city, around 7:15 a.m. Witnesses declared that they heard a great explosion before the Caravelle crashed. The plane dug an immense crater in the ground and debris has been recovered at considerable distances from the site of the accident. Fire spread to two neighbouring farms, but firemen quickly got the flames under control.

The company spokesman declared: "Everything

seemed normal upon take-off, but five minutes later we lost radio contact and the plane disappeared from our radar screens."

Among the seventy-two passengers were twenty-two couples from the village of Humlikon, who had gone to Geneva on a trip organized by the agricultural co-operative of the village. The accident thus leaves several children orphaned. An American, an Egyptian, an Israeli, an Iranian, and a Belgian were also on board.

Kloten airport confirms that weather was good when the plane took off and winds light.

"Do you see down there those little military planes . . . so slim, so polished, so closed in on themselves, very like sexual organs, in fact. Well, they're angels. Charlie, like God the Father, puts his angels in the sky and he makes them fly! *Oh Charlie you're so sweet!*"

It was nearly noon hour when we left the control tower. The others would already be on the Hillock.

"*If I found love in a motel, maybe my daughters (if I have any) will make love in a 'jetel' some day. . . .*"

She doesn't often pause and think tenderly of eventual children. She was set off by a few little girls in the street on the way home (unfolding their fingers they chanted *Eenie meenie*). Propped up in my arms in the depths of the overheated taxi, Patricia closes her eyes to the bright sun and hums some Broadway tunes.

18

And she had always wanted to sing during our games of love and chance, between our firm kisses and our slow breathing and our hands, which sought to read each other's body in braille. Twice, perhaps three times, we found each other again under the tepid shower. Already she had that habit of lathering the soap around her breasts, drawing symbols on her body, transforming herself into a Chinese billboard. In bed, the entire scores of "South Pacific" and "Porgy n' Bess" filled our night.

Stretched out in the sand the next morning, the heat dizzied us and flattened us against the sun. My gestures were thick and clumsy, like an ant caught in chewing-gum in the sun.

Patricia folded a dark blue kerchief over her eyes and offered her entire body to the light which burst from everywhere, white, white, white as if it had no intermediate shades, no ultra-whatever it is, as if in passing through the atmosphere it had lost all the tints we know it has in the spectrum. Raw, as if the sky had been cut from a celery-heart.

Around noon, our senses reeling from so much light and our bodies hot and moist, we didn't even have the courage to go into the lake (*the water is cold but once you're in . . .*). We went back to the cabin for a little coolness, our sandaled feet thumping along the painted wood sidewalk. We went to sleep together for the first time, on the freshly made bed. We spent the best of our time in that room, that long rectangle of looped-woolen carpet, sleeping or playing.

(Around noon, our senses reeling from so much light and our bodies cold and dry, we couldn't go to the Hillock. We returned to our room for warmth, our feet awkward in furry boots on the icy sidewalks that had hardly been touched by sand or salt.)

"And Madeleine?"

". . . ."

"Don't you want to answer?"

"There's no point."

"That fall, the Mounties came here, you. . . ."

"It doesn't surprise me."

"They suspected you of belonging to an international drug chain, or of having. . . ."

"That's ridiculous, you know it is!"

"*Who knows?*"

"Have they come back since?"

"No, I received a summons, then they cancelled it, and nothing since."

"How stupid it is! Life, real life! Your bed, your room, love, our trips, Madeleine, what nonsense! Jesus! Are you sure there's nothing for us to do anywhere, that's important, serious, worth doing? I dream of one day being able to forget myself. In the army I forgot because of sheer weariness, in these sheets I forget because of love and sleep, but I'll have to be able to forget . . . oh, what do I know about it . . . by doing nothing, or even.'. . ."

19

I wanted to tell her about the sea and the ideas I had one morning, drinking black, thick coffee at the Plaza Café in Veracruz; but Patricia falls asleep like a twelve-year-old dog, fighting vainly against the dropping of her eyelids, things revolve, grow dim, she sinks into sleep as soon as I talk to her about yesterday or life *out there*, the life I would have led without her. When she opened her eyes again, she dressed rapidly without saying a single word, then she shouted above the slam of the door behind her: "I'm going to the bank. We need money."

20

Outside the sun draws designs and draws patterns in the streets: here and there the pavement shows through the crusted snow, black (grey, if there's a wind), encircled with wet salt. Maybe spring will come in a single burst.

21

"Here! We can hang on for a few weeks yet."

"Is it your savings?"

"No, not really; just small change."

She shrugs, throws a bottle on the bed. *"Money means nothing. I have more than you can spend."*

"Doesn't it turn your stomach to have so much?"

Here we go, generous ideas, little Chinese children! I stuff myself while others starve themselves to death, maybe that's my problem; you are Capital and my people have suffered enough because of it. A daughter of the enemy is my mistress. Very *fin de siècle*, but how far will I take this romanticism?

That's not true: my compatriots eat their fill. But you can get stinking drunk and spit on them; your people are the stronger. Yes you will win, and yes we are cowards, Patricia, come undress yourself, come to bed, put out the light, make a void, I need the void of dark desire, come lick my hand.

22

On the ceiling intermittent spokes of light, first pear-shaped then knife-shaped, lengthening suddenly every time a car left King Street to lose itself on Lakeshore Drive in a screech of tires racked by speed, a sudden turn of the wheel, the heat of the macadam. The game of headlights, our lighted cigarettes which we used to make signs the way the technician on the airstrip makes signs (that incredible feeling of solitude I had early one morning on the cement airstrip in Glasgow, that man far off, his dark cap or beret on his head, his arms encased in incandescent gloves, calling in the planes the way we call birds), the gleam of an eye, the white of an eye sometimes, highlights in the thick darkness and silence. . . .

(Alone, to find yourself alone like a child abandoned by his team which won't let him play anymore, alone feeling the sharp, fresh wind and the scraped hills of Glasgow in Scotland, where they speak English, of course; they speak that language the whole world over, I have that little idiosyncrasy myself, thank you; you come from Canada? How do you keep from being American? *We have the same Queen*, murmured the man who sold cashmere sweaters duty free; the same Queen, my ass, leave that to *Paris Match*, we're not rebels, we're not alone against the Pentagon, and the House of Lords and good taste and the Republic and Westminster and Ottawa!)

Sunday at dusk, we had to go home like schoolchildren; the road stretched through fifty villages and the bus had to stop in each one, wait, start up again. I sat at the back, near the motor, my head against the window, and I drowsed. Patricia had to take the express, which alone stopped at Winnipeg. So that we'd be separated as little as possible, she had me buy a scarlet MG on credit at the end of August.

Selling copper shells was no longer enough, and I began to write some indiscreet commentaries about camp life, which I sold to the local weekly (*The Sentinel?*). Then I began to receive money from some people for not writing certain articles, and from some others, for being sure to mention them – all of which brought in three times the actual sale price of the articles themselves. . . . (Patricia never knew what miserable things I resorted to so I could pay for her whims, and had she known, she would have rejected me. All her life, money was familiar, necessary, natural. Her father – a Czechoslovakian Jew who established a chain of service stations – and her mother – an Irish textile heiress – had raised her in the solid luxury of security and beauty. Patricia added to this heritage a

certain taste for adventure and the natural carefree attitudes of her age. I came from a family of much more
modest means.)

We leisurely toured the Lake in the MG, going
first along the shopping streets, then via the traffic
circles and the boulevards; it was a subtle sort of game
in which one never knew – and was never supposed to
know – who was winning, the pedestrians or ourselves.
For us, the sights were on the sidewalks, those summer
merry-makers in sloppy shoes; for them it must have
been Patricia – nose and pink sunglasses to the wind,
finely moulded breasts under her apple-green sweater,
her head hidden under a large straw hat decorated with
a black velvet ribbon.

We were also part of a privileged group which met
at certain regular hours, following a well-established
curve of boredom, at a drive-in restaurant on the flank
of a hill to the north of the village. The group would
arrive by car or perhaps by horseback, but always by
following a mosquito-infested short cut through the
woods and hills.

Patricia was as changeable in this group as any
other adolescent, nervously laughing at everything, at
herself, at me. They called me Frenchie; we grimaced
as we emptied bottles of gin and scotch stolen by the
more audacious members of our group. We sat on the
running-boards of cars, hunched forward, clutching a
handful of pebbles warmed by the sun, never speaking
without shouting. And every now and then, a sham
scuffle, blows and shouts for nothing, over the name of
a highschool or college written on the back of a white
sweat shirt, over the number of pistons in a motor, over
the length of an average penis or rod.

(They all went home at the beginning of September, however, leaving the Lake to us, an immense
empty park, and that true silence of the false forest and
the united front of hotels closed in the glow of out-of-
season.)

23

We're both relaxed, rosy-faced: the bottle Patricia brought is empty, we're done with our primitive dances and, lying on our backs, breathing heavily, we shut our eyes.

Tires call out anxiously in the night, squeals to set your teeth on edge; you hear a car sliding on the ice, unable to make the incline by the Grenadier Guards; the impatient motorist races his engine, the wheels scream, and then another car stalls, others answer from the bottom, middle of the slope; sometimes, just barely audible, the continuous wail of a train going through the viaduct down below. . . .

(And in palm-leaf huts the wind made the parrots whistle; sometimes at daybreak nervous dogs kept me awake.)

24

Patricia, her eyes on the ceiling, smiles: "There's no game of lights here."

"If you close your eyes."

"There's no game. (Angry) You've come on a pilgrimage?" She rises on her side, her arm making a white triangle on the pillow. "You've come back to take up where you left off, or perhaps to light the lamp before leaving again?"

"I came back because it was winter. That's it."

(Not for the light or for winter: I was afraid of dying alone down there like a snake on the road, like a poisoned rat, drunk, gorged, ridiculous. I no longer knew where to go so, I came back here, it's simple. To regain contact with life, perhaps, with your body, to reknit yesterday and tomorrow. . . . I could no longer continue life with nothing but memories, incipient gestures, scraps of uneasiness.)

"You, uneasy?"

"Yes, me."

"You're joking, man."

I'm splitting my sides laughing, perhaps, but it's all inside: it grabs me in the eosophagus, it shakes the stomach, the pancreas, even my intestines are jumping. . . . I'm no longer a kid, and yet if a speaker begins to pontificate about the meaning of life, I listen religiously. Is there a part missing somewhere, am I missing one? Fine. I go, I live, I do things that are neither average nor petty, I die.)

"But the after-life is the craziest of all."

"You were saying?"

"I said the hell with angels."

Patricia rolls over on herself: she undressed tonight bit by bit, with an intense langour, as if she had to seduce me or die. She presses against me once again, uses the attachment of luxurious flesh, falls back on the sheet, plays dead, then slowly comes to, a long quiver in the belly, uncurls herself, complains, balks.

She plays, gets up, lights a cigarette, throws away the package, scarcely looks at me, amused: "I was married last spring."

"I didn't know."

"To an Englishman. From London or Liverpool. I never asked him anyway; he went off on our honeymoon alone, in a BOAC plane."

"You didn't love him anymore?"

"No."

"And then?"

"No consequences: I menstruated that month as usual. I married him to strengthen my Anglo-Saxon roots, so. . . ."

"And then?"

"Ties are a nuisance: they trip you up."

(*Falling down falling down. . . .*)

30

Patricia runs from the bedroom to the living room flapping her wings like a fleeing chicken; then she comes back with a serious face, contrite even, coils into my arms, around my hips, makes herself a little girl.

"We should have met sooner."

"That summer?"

"No, I mean, four years old. *Nursery rhyme* age. How do you say *nursery rhyme* in French?"

"*Comptines. Un deux trois quatre ma petite vache a mal aux pattes.*"

"Jack and Jill went up the hill to fetch a pail of water."

"*Belle pomme d'or je tire ma révérence.*"

"Eenie meenie minie moe, Catch a nigger by the toe, If he. . . ."

"Hey! We recited that one too."

"For hide-and-seek?"

"I think so. My mother taught it to us when desserts were rare and we had to choose without using the short-straw method: nursery rhymes are useful, to choose a dessert or a scapegoat.

(I'm afraid I'll die suddenly, I'm afraid, there, in the pit of my stomach, to kick off without having made a single human gesture, without leaving behind me something other than my stiffening body, my rotting body, my humus in the rock and the clay; you remember that stupid accident. A week in hospital. Our anxiety: the green cement walls, the signs at the doors (*The Royal*) ordering silence, the elevator, the metallic sound of the oiled doors, the bored look of the interns: your head on the pillow, your white hair – you had just bleached it – the flowers above the chair where I spent three days afraid you'd never open your eyes again.)

Today I'm alive, everyone knows I'm alive. Tomorrow I die: Who will know that I ever existed?

"The news vendor, by God!"

"You don't understand. . . ."

"*Man at this time of night one should either drink or make love!*"

The sheets flew back and Patricia ran to the window, her body rigid. The wan colour of a night of pallid snow filtered in through the window to make a nude rectangle, like old, polished marble. Her body leaning toward the day, motionless, dreams, then it is back-lit in the increasing light, a dark, drowsing silhouette.

(I shouldn't really annoy her like that.)

3

25

September came, like a fair to set up, silent in its still-shuttered booths, its flattened, rolled-up canvas; like a marketplace on Monday morning, empty and peaceful; arborite counters and metal struts, waiting for something to support, dead leaves lining the road (even under balconies, piled up by the night wind, probably).

We still went to the Holiday Motel, even if scarcely ten tourist couples were left and the entire population of the lake had deserted the oasis at the beginning of the month. We still arrived Thursday night, in the rain; wet leaves on the road made the car skid at every turn; it took two hands on the wheel and constant gearing down in order to hold the road, then suddenly, impossibly, warning lights and a quick veer to the road shoulder.

The white line straight down the middle of the asphalt hypnotized me; a fascinating road in white and black: if I was sleepy, Patricia sang aloud, told me the ironies of the week and the current big excitement at the university. She told me about her Monday-morning flirtations, when she'd stroll the campus the way prostitutes stroll Rue Saint-Denis. She manipulated me from the depths of her imagination, two words from her could make me tender or jealous. We'd arrive at the lake so exhausted that we often seemed strangers to each other.

26

It's so clear in my mind: We'd sleep to mid-morning on Friday, then spend the rest of the day on horseback, riding through the gardens, the parks, the fields, which until yesterday were still *Private Property* (neat square white signs, black letters), galloping, trotting, leaping fences, ploughing up fragile grass until the black earth broke through.

And the autumn air so cool, the horses hardly sweated.

(Sometimes, we hunted wild ducks and Canada Geese which used the Lake as a stop-over point on their slow trip to the Southern United States. But it meant getting up very early. Inside a blind, a gun between our knees, we'd drink cognac from a thermos bottle, watching the sun rise and feeling increasingly part of an incredibly human universe, extravagantly ours. Ours right down to the cry of the orioles, the starlings, the thrush, down to the wind whistling high in the branches of the blue spruce, down to the taste of the cigarette that seemed our only source of warmth, and the unsuccessful rifle shot and the noise of wings like hurrying footsteps, a dizzying flight, the dog-like cry of geese whose throats were angry with rust.)

At night we'd join the other survivors, vacationers, and proprietors resting after the holidays, in the dark, dirty Chinese grill (decorated with bamboo junks that would never make another voyage, bolted fast to the ceiling and filled with artificial flowers). The movie house was through for the season, so were the organized dances, the hot beach were everyone had gravely wandered about. Alone, a few beings joined together in tacit solidarity; alone, an unspoken agreement to meet at a fixed time in the Nanking Café; alone, sentences hanging in the air like cigarillo smoke.

I don't think we ever really talked together, hammered out a question, even argued politics. How could we, when we came from nowhere? We were scattered in a country of such vast space, such wide horizons that we only came to rest seated around a table in a Chinese restaurant, on the pretext of playing cards over steaming cups of coffee. Finally we relaxed, face to face, the Polish worker, the Ukrainian farmer, the Hun engineer, and the Brazilian hairdresser, the Scottish pastor,

Patricia, and me the French Canadian, and Carl the salesman; we were the whole of Canada gathered around a rectangle of yellow linoleum in an atmosphere heavy with fried food and cherry sauce. Mute. Monosyllabic.

(I had only one consolation: By cheating a little at cards, I managed to win enough money in one evening to pay the motel bill for the entire stay, and then some.)

We left the table to walk quickly across the park to our room, to make love, to feel the warm water of the shower. (Once I cheated on Patricia with the Brazilian. She led me to her room on a pretext of violent indigestion and then appeased her indecent hunger by nibbling my sexual parts like celery. To get even, I up-ended her on a thoroughly uncomfortable arm-chair, then fled when she went into the washroom. Patricia was still waiting for me at the restaurant, we ate egg rolls in silence, she hummed American hits, told me that she dreamed of living in New York some day, or maybe Chicago (it was nearer), that she was simply *dying* to rub elbows with people, millions of men and women in an over-populated city, that the Chinese in fact. . . .)

27

A sudden storm has flattened the city: a few hours have transformed streets into soft fields of snow. Huge nests of snow cling to the forks of trees on the windward side, garland passers-by with identical hats: asexual beings advance in a sort of white fog, fighting the wind, straining their whole bodies in an effort that the ice under foot promptly nullifies. Silent.

These people are silent all winter. When summer comes, they've forgotten how to speak. The fight is very simple: not to be cold. Some drink hot gin, others sleep, hibernate in the heart of the year.

We are still naked, cosy under five blankets, but Patricia rages against the storm: neither of us has the courage to get up and close the window where the wind is rushing in, building up a miniature iceberg on the rug that even the heat of the radiator can't melt.

"Will you take me to eat sunshine and pastry if I get up and close the window?"

Patricia came back to bed with her hands full of snow, threw it in my face, under the sheets. The snow instantly melted on our bodies; I drank the water from her shoulder, and on her icy skin I tried to merge with her boiling blood.

"All this is frivolous, ridiculously *frivolous*! We're so *fragile,* there are so many serious things we should be concerned with, so much fascism! Say, I think I'll become a highway robber, kiss me." (I'll die, I know, I'll die tonight or another morning perhaps, but more and more I'm harassed by the image of the child I was and am no longer: I'm growing *old*, I'm used up, they're crossing my hands on my chest, they're reciting prayers at my back, they're sobbing as if. . . .)

. . . Patricia is a depth of pleasures: she groans with joy as soon as I enter her (it's not death so much that frightens me as the thought of leaving *all this unfinished.* My good intentions and my evil thoughts, my love and my political choice, what am I here for; it's not my country any longer, was it ever? Once I'm satisfied, Patricia is only a memory, what a strange world. . . .)

"Are you getting dressed?"

And *that*, in the pit of the stomach, what is it? Fear, the great bitch fear, all the garbage, the hole in front of you: To be useless, I am useless, you are useless.

"I'm waiting for you."

Tic-toc-tic-toc. The next war won't need me: I'll

become a cook; I prefer potatoes to being burned alive;
the flame-throwers of an indifferent enemy are not for
me; peelings, cabbage soup, too bad for the homeland,
I like radishes better.

29

Outside: snow. You make a hole inside, as if to
enter an igloo and then suddenly you tumble into the
heart of Italy.

"Do you remember the postcards?"

We spent a whole Friday in the Holiday Motel
looking over a collection of postcards her father had
given her. Patricia told me about cities, monuments
(obelisks like petrified missiles), the colour of stones,
and the intensity of the heat, as if she had lived her
entire life in Asia or Europe. We made up battles, pilgrimage sites, city plans. We made love that morning
in Tokyo; that afternoon in Berlin; and Patricia sang in
German until we fell upon a card of Vancouver. Already, alas, we were back in Canada.

30

I had an absurd nightmare: someone, perhaps
an enemy or an Indian god or simply a water serpent,
had pulled the plug, and the Lake, naked and dry,
offered up its slimy belly to bewildered passers-by. Cat-
fish agonized here and there, their flanks heaving. Little
by little, the ooze took on the imprints of trout and pike,
as if the depths of the Lake had met the open sky to

become an illustrated page of past ages. (Ours, this time.)

31

Autumn grew drier, the light shorter, and only the green fir needles brought memories of heat and water. We often left the car in a deserted lane and took a walk, side by side, hands in pockets, for we were preoccupied with the existence of God: the discussion was better on foot, we were more at ease, enjoying the exquisite pleasure of dawdling, happy in the sunlight suddenly flashing between over-thick, soap-sudsy clouds. As we talked we chewed on stalks of rye-grass. We found excitement in telephone poles, trees, fence-posts, pleasure in our easy speech with each other, pride in our supple, powerful bodies. We were preoccupied with ourselves, our muscles alert.

And, to increase already intense pleasure, I had memories of similar walks on the leafy paths and dirt roads you find all along the St. Lawrence, down-stream from Sorel, near the little white and green house my parents had those two long-ago summers. But the feeling of *déjà vu*, of *déjà senti* (that sudden vertiginous sensation you sometimes get from an illustration: a photo of yesterday, of a place you couldn't have known yet as familiar as your own childhood), a trembling lip because of a colour already seen somewhere else, before, yesterday, an identical noise. . . . That autumn, my sensitivity was ten-fold.

And Patricia, so beautiful, so in harmony (harmonious Patricia, they should have taken the proportions of the ideal figure from your body), her cheeks slightly rosy, her make-up still properly matte-finished despite the wind; with some difficulty she quoted the Gide they had taught her in French grammar lessons.

She talked aloud about a Supreme Being. My only concern, I think, was for her.

32

And also at the end of September, I decided to abandon the Camel and his regiment. Fine. They had taught me to fire certain guns according to an ideal triangle and two sighting-marks. But the chief result of my sojourn in the service of Canada was a strong aversion to trigonometry and the colonial spirit. Having dipped into my pay – and that of a few friends distracted by alcohol – I changed my uniform for a black-and-white striped suit. I headed for the refuge of the city. Patricia easily persuaded me to live with her, delighted to have me entirely at her disposal – as much for the help with her French lessons as for the night-time satisfaction of her burgeoning sexuality.

33

October came. I was bored stiff in those monotonous streets – all the more so because I hadn't any money – in this mediocre city where you can't tell downtown from the suburbs, for all the rusty red bricks are alike. And then the drizzle, the smoke in the fog, the sullen air of a naked-faced crowd, without privilege, without love. . . .

One Thursday we went back to the oasis, but the water in the Lake was already frozen around the rocks; the rowboats were pulled up on the sand and turned over like toys; green wooden shutters blanked every window. Nothing left: dead leaves, a few chipmunks burying useless nuts, a bored watchman. We left the same evening.

The next morning, I sold my car, bought Patricia a ring, and before the Weekend Garage could tell me I still had eighteen payments to make, I decided to leave. Obviously, I invited her to follow me to Montreal; she bit into the project like buttered toast.

Either her parents took me for what I wasn't (Patricia had passed me off as a visiting professor at the university) or else they were eager to get rid of her so easily (how could they believe I was a professor when I looked so much more like a student), but in any event they promptly granted her request to enroll at McGill and in some private language or music or even dramatic arts course at a specialized school in Montreal. They really didn't give a damn, and neither did we.

It was a feverish Saturday. Patricia bought shoes, skirts, blouses, suits, sweaters, coats at random – more prudent than I, she left the bills for her father. She led us from one shop to another, from one taxi to . . . etc.

(A moment ago she asked me what I intended to do, if I was going to settle down, reside, work perhaps. I told her I had no idea, that I certainly wasn't going to join any nine-to-five office, come home with a paper in my hand like a dog with a bone in his jaw . . . but it's still the city of dreams: 100,000 offices are looking for a pencil-pusher to sit under fluorescent lights and add up life-insurance premiums, or fire-insurance, theft, automobile, accident, disaster, frost. These security-hungry people pay their little green coupons faithfully, and the little green coupons build these strange cement skyscrapers timidly pockmarked with windows, which in turn enslave the people, for the money is immediately reinvested in industrial development, and there we are full circle: exploited workers eager for security, pay . . . but no. Scribbling under the neon, eighty-five dollars a week . . . never! Well, not now. I'll pluck daisy petals and choose the right thing in time, *Eenie, meenie, minie, moe.*

It's not that I'm afraid of work. When there was a drought in the village, I drew up an irrigation plan like ones I had seen in movies, and I helped Indians build canals, ditches, sluice-gates, approaches, distribution gutters and flowing gutters, immense conduits. Six weeks under the dry blue sky, dusty, slowly establishing the gradients, the basins, the fall of the water; slavery, all in all. . . .)

(But I dream of yielding, especially today; I would like to be obliterated like those cars they squeeze into blocks of metal, into a compact mass in an automatic crusher; I would like to crawl. Always this spasm, here, in the pit of the stomach which. . . .)

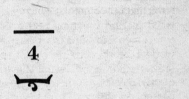

4

In the sleeping cars, the black porters in their red caps decked in gold braid held back the khaki curtains, lifted the seats, punched up the pillows, unfolded the naphthalene-scented blankets with precise, efficient gestures, rather like a knife blade sinking in . . . razor-like movements; the train, from Vancouver, was spending two hours in the station that Sunday evening, carrying letters and newspapers, livestock as well. Time stretched out, smells grew thick; we stood on the oiled wood platform, patient and watchful, waiting for the train's signal to shine from the heart of the tunnel. They worked in the puffing steam, checking ice, wheels, brakes, oil pressure. I would have liked to spend the rest of my days right there, in pre-departure. The other passengers shivered, perhaps uneasy or perhaps simply unaccustomed to the sudden gusts of air that blasted between the coaches. Patricia was happy, headed for adventure in full security, her father would support her with a generous allowance. Me. . . .

(I feel *tonight*, perhaps for the first time, that I will leave again. I don't know if Patrica will be with me; nor what kind of trip it will be, but suddenly I perceive (like a piercing cry in the ear) the necessity for departure. At best, she and I, we have a certain complicity between us, memories; as if each of us held half the pieces of a Chinese puzzle which I must at any price complete. I also feel – despite myself – a question of:

"You call that living?"

"What more do you want?"

"I'm wearing myself out, my muscles and my spirit, my eyes; but I want it to be for someone, for something!"

"All you have to do is produce babies."

"Stupid broad!"

And you, Patricia, will you be able to keep yourself what you now are, a page pulled from between the covers of *Seventeen*, and yet become a woman, a useful woman. . . .)

35

We're lying one on top of the other in little super-imposed caskets, and I don't hear her say a word. I don't know if she fell asleep as soon as she stretched out or if – like me – she's looking through a slit in the blinds at the passing night, pursued by fires, houses, the double headlights of cars trying to cross the railway tracks, and then suddenly, the enormous black nothing-ness in which you can see a few tree-tops or a thicket of trees, here, there, a stand of birch or trembling poplar, and then nothing. A few minutes from the city, and already we're in the middle of the desert with a selection of trees, in *space*, on the savannah.

The steady, brittle clicking of wheels against tracks finally swayed the coach into such pure rhythm that I fell into deep sleep – surely exhaustion – dividing my night between a new emotional vacuum and a per-sistent, regressive nightmare in which I set myself the task of populating the surrounding land, crossing Europe, making speeches in the public squares of France and Holland that armed men were always brutally interupting, dispersing the attentive peasants with blows and kicks; I was babbling: *"America waits for you, liberty holds out her arms to you, solitude calls you, you will sleep in the trees, and eat teals, larks, and swallows . . . ."* And then for no reason I suddenly woke up, or perhaps there was a shift in the rhythm of the coach, or a mechanical signal had begun to pierce the night ding-ding-ding, automatic rattles, some level crossings, or yet again the emptiness suddenly making itself felt like a profound uneasiness, when the speed-ing train crossed over a river and the noise reverberated in the echoing depths of the bridge.

Five o'clock sunlight yanked me from the nightmare which had reclaimed me, just as the boats laden with colonists were leaving Saint Malo. . . . I couldn't shut my eyes, yet my fatigue refused to go away, I was exhausted enough to believe in hallucinations. I lay there wilted, panting. Far off, behind a curtain of poplars, you could make out a road which would soon be streaming with the people who carry civilization from city to village, Fuller brushes, Simpson's Sears catalogues. I dressed as best I could, folded in two to pull on slacks and shoes. Patricia was still sleeping, smiling, unconscious. I stationed myself on the platform between two coaches, protected by the dirty brown curtains, immersed in the infernal racket, and sucking in the air, despite the soot.

(Is it possible? We're leading parallel lives like ski tracks in the snow, I tell myself; going to such and such a station with such and such a person, taking a path similar to another person's, or alone, making the same gestures again and believing they're new, when they've hardly even been remodelled. Like ten, forty, a hundred-million cars on a multi-lane, multi-level speedway, we pass, rejoin, meet at the greasy spoons – I hold my fork the same way whether I eat with Patricia or someone else! – then back to the road, full . . . knowing perfectly well that the gestures of love, and hate, and boredom, or even adventure, are always the same. . . .

(Illusions have a short life; whether in décor [it's all a matter of . . .] Italian or Armenian, or heat, or noise, I lose myself bit by bit in deep hallways . . . and in the snowy streets swept with winds from the four corners of the city, covering all, even the nasal cries of the loud-speakers with their seasonal melodies and little clinking bells, "Rudolph, the Red-nosed Reindeer," since Christmas, since the new year, since the child I used to be and would so much like to be again, trusting.)

Pressed against the partition, I had trouble keeping myself upright as the coaches lurched along, especially on curves, but like a stubborn cat in a corner, I breathed in the fresh air, autumn, the perfume of burned leaves on the embankments. Narrow bands of landscape frayed themselves on the distorted screen formed by the door and the half-lowered window: And the pounding speed welded the fuzzy objects into astonishing unity; the thin colours of a few maples splattered the sombre depths of fir and spruce; farther back a few solitary pines, clusters of cedar and larch stuck in the earth like random tent posts, hid rusty earth covered now in green, now in grey moss.

Patricia got up in time (even so) to drink coffee with me in the buffet of a miniscule train station which would have astonished Alice In, while railwaymen used the ten minutes pause to top up water and fuel. We could have been anywhere at all, or somewhere else: those neutral shades spread on the walls like old newspapers glued behind wallpaper, the oily taste of the coffee-cream, of flour in the white bread, right down to the penmanship of the menu . . . and in the strange light that came through the dirty window like blue eyeshadow, you could see over the counter to the road from Saskatoon which stopped before a monument to the dead (*Lest We Forget 1914-1918 the Valiant Lads Who* . . .), a pious city councillor surely must have added the names of soldiers wiped out in the next war (*Lest We Forget 1939-1945*) and two or three names of kids my age who died in the war that never was (*Clarence Campbell, David Bairstow, Michael Petrusky, Died in Korea on the Fourth of November 1951*) . . . farther on cement stairs, like drugstore lozenges, like tiers in a stadium, leading to the shops overlooking Victoria Square. Lower down you could see the white wooden columns (Doric) of the Masonic Temple, or perhaps the Canadian Legion (spotless rooms where ladies of no particular age or elegance go Saturday afternoon to knit socks for children-in-need, and their husbands go Saturday night to drink a little too much over religion or politics, or the ass on the minister's daughter)....

An insect buzzed in the waiting room, knocked against the window, eager for light, raising the dust, sinking, stirring again....

Somnolent, my head against the leather backrest of the seat, yielding little by little to the serene numbness of wheel against rail, accepting the rhythm, I suddenly saw the sky between my lashes and my nose like a gigantic fly's wing delicately posed against a blue and grey backdrop, vibrating nervously, newly torn from the stellar body....

An insect buzzed in the waiting room and, seeking the light, rushes headlong into the window-pane; it stirred up dust, hurt itself, and then began its search again....

37

"I'm famished, starved, that's it."

"Maybe you don't eat enough."

"*Don't be ridiculous, Patty.*"

"You're all *exhausted*, you French, whether you come from France, Quebec, or Navarre . . . you're sick over the fact that you didn't invent the civilization of the twentieth century, so you mumble in your corner like little old ladies in a Home. . . ."

"There's so much to save."

"Go to it, Christian! You want to save everything, go on, Jansenist!"

"Maybe you're right."

"Just wait: Soon there'll be a new *earthly* adventure, you'll be at ease then, more than the Turks. . . ."

"Why do you say that? Why the *Turks*?"

"Because I'm fed up with your shrunken skin, your suddent outbursts of moralism, your continual lament, your groaning, and above all, your *ideas*."

Our feet like ice, our toes curled up in fur boots, we go on tramping about in the snow, going around in circles (I'll get a terrible cold if this keeps up), bit by bit the Problem emerges: if only I had a black skin, a Jewish nose! Theirs are great cultures, known the world over! I speak French in America, that's *the* sin, the crime, if I were the bastard son of the Folies-Bergères and Paris by Night, the Salvation Army couldn't be any more scandalized. . . .

But I'm not scandalized by myself any more; *the time-span of an adolescence* . . . Patricia begins to run down toward the Fairlaine Bookstore where we'll amuse ourselves pulling out the most bizarre of the American paperbacks.

38

Behind us a gentleman says: "Autumn only has meaning in this country, where winter and summer are both so exaggerated. . . ."

The train window offers us a semi-coloured landscape, the white bark of the tree clusters, the dry skin of the elms, the sleek peelings of the maples.

"Wolves! I think so. Or grey dogs!"

But the train moved too quickly for us to be sure. Anyway, no one has yet seen those forests: on foot, the undergrowth is so dense that you can't tell a hare from a clump of moss at two paces. The perfect place to lose yourself, or bring down a hunter with a misplaced shot. Only the lakes, sometimes. . . .

"All this comfort, these plastic domes, the sole *à l'anglaise*."

"In Europe the trains aren't as luxurious or as big. . . ."

"But they have the essential element for a trip: the unexpected, the surprise of meeting a passenger who knows everything about the intimate life of Pliny the Elder or how they built the Carousel gratings in the Palais du Louvre."

"Darling, your weakness for quiz games always astonishes me."

"That's not it: This scene lacks relief, that's all, and I don't like one dimension."

"*But that is true of everywhere in this land; it's true of everyone. You. Me. Imagine! For instance, I was eight. . . .*"

Bit by bit we exchanged our childhoods, like two kids exchanging tokens, pictures, keys, foreign coins.

I tried to interject her stream of rich-girl memories with my cramped little scenes, set in a small corner of the countryside, in summer, or in a flowery kitchen (flowers painted everywhere, even on the door of the stove) through the long winters, where my father glued his ear to the radio and followed the advances and retreats of the Allied troops, as if the battles were taking place under our windows. He dreamed of politics, I think, without ever doing anything about it, but he was an honest man and his world-conscience (of the *deserts*) left him more preoccupied with campaigning soldiers than with the problems civilians had to solve.

I was ten: At that moment America chose to transform her automobile factories into assembly lines for cannons and tanks, which she built with a cigar between her lips, part greed and part kindness. Every effort was a war effort, and the city was plastered with billboards where Churchill, wrinkled brow, debonnair eyes, and the V sign, talked to us in English (*give us the tools and we'll finish the job*), which was enough to send sturdy guys of twenty fleeing into the woods, they didn't want to fight, not they. But this war didn't leave us with legless cripples, armless cripples, orphans, or men with surgical holes in their skulls: it merely sowed in us the first germs of uneasiness, suspicion . . . the adults said: They've bombarded Dunkirk, but nothing happened around us, no fireworks, no searchlights fingering the clouds, no anti-aircraft fire, nothing, nothing but uneasiness like a balloon slowly, imperceptibly swelling. Nothing except, occasionally, in certain families, a wounded son flown back from Italy via London, like luggage.

39

It's still snowing; powdery, blinding, white gusts of snow. . . . We've come back from the Hillock to be swallowed up in a tiny theatre in the business district where "Duel in the Sun," which we had seen that summer at the Lake, was trying to arouse the passions of the average Protestant: For three days Patricia has been dragging me to the theatre, silent, as if she had suddenly been struck with a strange malady. The day before yesterday, she cried out: "*I hate too much. I love too much. That is the trouble: too much. I'm sick of it all!*"

Since then she hasn't stirred, not one muscle in her face has moved, she answers with onomatopoeia, she scarcely looks at me; yes it's a trick, surely a trick to make me, alone with myself, decide everything. Or has she really chosen to live, a recluse, insulated from my fretfulness?

40

Around noon we saw the sun force its way obliquely through the closed windows, casting dusty shadows through the coach. As we moved east, there were more cities, smokier and duller, with their narrow streets where neon lights shone all day, pink and yellow on their brick foundations.

Naturally, the train passed through the hearts of these towns, which were spun out along their life-blood, the railway line. The railway line was the one nervous system of possible life (today the plane). . . .

We looked down from our plush seats and half-heartedly played the American tourist, waving at children who had come to see the train pass; but really, *we* were the children, especially Patricia. One moment she was at my side, the next she was on the opposite chair, her legs tucked under her supple wool dress the colour of hot dry sand. She began little dissertations she never finished, pointing at heads with her finger, describing factories and the baroque architecture of the 1920's . . . we weren't the least bit concerned about our neighbours, who seemed as intrigued by our freewheeling gestures as by our shocking conversations, sure that we were too young for a honeymoon, be it to the mountains or Niagara Falls (because we couldn't fit into their plans of birth-engagement-marriage-death, they rejected us like a spent cigarette, snuffed out, already cold).

The horizon jiggled, the trees fled. Soon the only noise was the train, its buggy hammering the rails, and the voices or tears of a few children as their families filed one after the other to the dining-car.

We passed the time between cities the way we'd pass it in church, making up sacred places, forbidden places, unexpected noises: The corridor became at will a convent hallway, a hospital wing, the entrance to a cell, the narrow bridge where Aladdin had to wait (without touching the wall, on pain of death – despite the jostlings of the train), the underground room hiding the marvellous lamp shaped like a Swedish sauce-boat; or, a game of nine-pins which took in three whole coaches, and all this wrapped in the cries of birds, a mixture of thrush, titmouse, nightjar, hummingbird, jay, starling, and especially the raucous mockery of the crow (the last squawk) fleeing southward for the season (the

quetzal, a sacred bird, which the children in the village
used to feed with special seeds). . . .

41

The projector crackled behind the dusty window
of the projection room, and its light, continually vary-
ing in intensity with the opacity of the colour being
thrown, certainly interested me more than that dread-
ful short on trout-fishing in Lake-Louise-Mirror-of-the-
Rockies; the American newsreel showed us an aircraft
carrier where student pilots learned to set down little
machines that were already obsolete for war; then the
Brazilian embassy, where the most beautiful women
stayed at the gate, their eyes feverish and their hands
tense. Patricia is rigid indifference in the shadows, like
a faulty barometer relegated to a spot above a useless
dresser.

42

We were to arrive in Montreal in the early morning. Patricia wanted us to stay up so that we wouldn't
miss anything of the night, awake to enjoy every stop,
visit every station. The moon – exceptionally clear and
distinct – reflected enough light to transform the countryside into phosphorescent landscapes and intrigue
our imaginations – already churning – into designing
undergrowth that would have done credit to a Shake-
spearian play.

Patricia chose to wear slacks and a dark leather
jacket so that she wouldn't be chilly in the night. We
hugged each other close and stood in the half-shut door-

way, leaping onto the platforms before the train had come to a complete halt, like important travellers hurry-to settle vital questions. At first the black porter tried to stop us but soon, discouraged, he let us have our way, preferring to drowse near the hot-air vent in the room next to the W.C. Almost all the stations were of burned brick, deep-furrowed, or else oiled brown wood, with a single gothic window for both tickets and information; a door with shelves for left-luggage, with sliding panels, two or three benches (which could have served in a chapel) placed in the middle of a tiny waiting-room, out of all proportion with the hours that men, women, and children had to spend there each day, and then that counter where an old lady – white hair, drooping breast, her dress fastened at the neck with a sparkling brooch – always the same, always the same age (we told our-selves: Surely it's the same old woman, she must sneak on board the train, then leap off and run behind the counters of dried-out cakes just a few seconds ahead of us; we tried to be quicker the next time; in vain, but) who sold pallid café au lait the colour of a river after a rainstorm, Sunkist oranges, propaganda comics and others that weren't as funny, a few day-old news-papers. . . .

Patricia shone with beauty in those dismal places and indulged almost every whim. I'm sure she dazzled each of those simple Canadian National functionaires, starchy in their Waterman blue uniforms with caps like French generals. They spent their time – that is, their train time – sizing her up the way a peasant sizes up an animal at auction that he knows he can't afford. So Patricia behaved like a trollop, laughing too loud too long, hanging on my neck like a garland of flesh (about two o'clock sleepiness encircled her eyes, her face softened like a charcoal sketch; sometimes, her eyes shut; suddenly motionless in the middle of a room or on the platform, she would cock an ear as if to hear the distant strains of jazz . . . discreet, muted, serene, hers alone . . . as if it were familiar to her: the breath of the ground, the wind, the . . .).

However, that trip gave us a two-day course in the geography of the provinces, sometimes pretentious, sometimes poetic, sometimes ridiculous, sometimes loving: Belle Plaine, Medicine Hat, Qu'Appelle, Val Marie, Foremost, Assiniboia, Lethbridge, Kennedy, Neepawa, Sandy Lake, Wawanesa, Jordanie, Paris, Laugneth, Polar Point, Manitou, Oxbow, Carman, Lac du Bonnet, Steinbach, Sundown, Crystal City, Montmartre, Kipling, Souris, Marienthal, Browning, Eden, Detroit, Port Huron, Chatham, London, Waterloo, Damascus, Nottawasaga, Port Credit, Hamburg, Frankford, Belleville, Toronto, Ottawa, Kingston, Iroquois, Long Sault. . . .

43
〰

I cherish the gentled curve of her shoulder, I love the dry curve of her hip as well, the spring. . . . [That sudden rain, of water, water everywhere, the earth became viscous, the adobe good and the bird-serpent happy; Manuello, the invalid, made love to Agnes when the storm broke; I slept, at least I think I slept; next to me the young Indian who kept my house wove banana leaves (in the eyes of her family, I had full rights); and she showed me a tenderness that was unusual at her age: At thirteen, she bought back the honey of her body by cheekily plundering the kitchen to the profit of her family, soon after the entire village, the stream.]
Today the streams are frozen, the sheets frozen, Patricia has crushed herself against me to get warm, trying to find a position that will allow her to sleep and soak up my body-heat at the same time. I don't know why: Suddenly I think of Jack London's dogs then, reminding myself that she had surely never read his books, of the romances of the Countess de Ségur, then La Fontaine's fables (surely an association between her

curled-up position and that of animals), yesterday's songs, Patricia holds me by the tip of my heart, ties me to her, *if he hollers let him go*, I'll holler some day, I'll cry out, like a Negro, with fire, one day, wait my God, from the cup to the lip. . . .

44

We were still up at four-thirty in the morning, when the conductor walked through the train, whispering in front of each berth that there was one hour of travelling left. To get things moving, the porter studiously began to make a great racket: Here was the start of an unwonted spectacle of dirty feet and red-painted toenails and black hair pushing through, dancing, shoving aside the ill-attached curtains; here a single leg, as if one of the travellers had been transformed into a flamingo, there the paw of a hippopotamus.

Each tried to work enough water out of a stingy tap to brush his teeth, shave, or simply comb his hair; only Patricia and I noticed the brown smoke scatter and reveal the birth of a city from its wide, empty suburban boulevards to its narrower, darker streets, as if the buildings had put themselves in order for a family portrait: from smallest to largest, in order of birth.

(Inside the coach, all was the creaking of hinges, forced, pinched, and stuck, the noise of bags banging against seats, nervous triggering of locks snapping shut, raucous shouts.)

The soot was thicker, like foliage in a forest, and the train went abruptly underground into a long white tunnel which led into the heart of the city beating faintly at the break of day. We had to recuperate from one hundred hours of train and landscape.

Here was: The station – as big as a new concert hall –where the music of arrival consisted of footsteps, metallic sounds of shutting racks, the bumpy echo, shouts from the loudspeakers.

Here was: A stairway rolling around itself, a conveyor following the rhythm of its belt and indifferently dropping laymen, priests, military men into a too-large room, all of them exhausted by the trip, surprised to walk on solid ground again, unable to find their accustomed pace.

Here was: The baggage encircling us; Patricia collapsing with weariness; and for me that city to tame once again after such a long absence.

Here was: The rusty black taxi, parasites on the radio, tips, an eighteen-step stairway, fatigue, heavy sleepiness in a day that was only beginning to live, in that city which was not a stranger to me.

5

The night doesn't really exist: It's semi-day, semi-dark (undoubtedly because of the abundant snow covering the houses to their roofs, the trees as well, shrouding cars and fences).

A city weighed down by the thickness of the frost and snow, yet at the same time light and airy under its blanket of white, powdery as chalk. Once again tonight dangerously overheated houses will burn like torches, like Buddhists in the four corners of the world.

Norwalk (AFP) – Sixty-three people lost their lives in a fire last Saturday which razed a retreat house for the old and infirm. There were twenty-four survivors.

Only twelve hours after the firemen had mastered the blaze, sixty-two bodies had been retrieved from the ruins and taken to a near-by school. Forty-seven of them have been officially identified and two claimed by relatives of the defunct. They are still looking for one body.

The fire, which did an estimated $100,000 worth of damage, totally destroyed the Golden Age home, situated in Lakeville, a resort centre 15 miles south-east of Norwalk.

At the height of the blaze, two passers-by risked their lives to save some old people from the flames who were too sick or feeble to walk. These two heroes are Henry Dahman, a taxi driver from Sarber, and Clifford French, 21, from Michigan, United States.

Four of the 24 survivors are in critical condition in hospital. The cause of the tragedy is unknown.

(I try to explain to her that, in the wooden homes of Abitibi and the Gaspé, it's usually children who burn like paper cut-outs.)

A moment ago, everything was normal. And then suddenly crisis, as if we had transformed ourselves into enemy birds. Patricia fumes, I shriek, we're upright on the dining-room table with burning eyes, then suddenly it stops, the shouts, and the strange sensation of being about to take off.

Maybe we should laugh.

Patricia cries.

It wasn't my intention to torment her like that; if she's upset, it hasn't been my doing. She says she can easily see herself leaping from a twenty-three-storey building in Regina, driven by wind and fury, no longer knowing how to fly, and being crushed like a pumpkin on the icy pavement.

What's left for me to stir up?

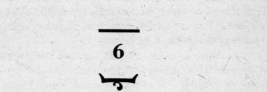

6

Patricia usually stayed in the house in Montreal, only going out for her late-afternoon courses. We had rented a sunny, five-room flat looking out on Mountain Street and backing on an automatic parking garage where gigantic elevators carried Cadillacs, Pontiacs, Olds, and Chryslers (most of them belonging to American tourists) top to bottom, six stories.

They work at break-neck speed, and we heard clackings, booming, hollow noises, amplified by the elevator shafts, an almost continual vibration which was most noticeable in the kitchen.

Patricia often played earthquake, shouting: "Hello! Hello! This is San Francisco, the first buildings are crumbling, twenty-six thousand people dying, their chests crushed by bricks and dislodged stones! Stay tuned to this station for further information and detailed reports, don't miss the earthquake. . . ."

The garage was shut every Sunday, giving us a few hours of solid ground. We felt a void in our life, like a (parenthesis) in our days. Moreover, the heart of the city was troubling at certain times: sleep cannot blend with that much silence.

Our love continued navel to navel.

Throughout November, until the beginning of December, we lived for ourselves; we'd walk through the districts whole nights at a time or take a bus to the outskirts; we went to the shores of the St. Lawrence, to Rivière des Prairies, to dream, talk, talk some more.

Sometimes I'd take her to streets that were familiar to me, describe them to her, saying: "We used to play here when I was eight, ten maybe – in the gardens down there; every old man in the area had his plot, and we used to steal vegetables and eat them raw, and then over there: The rocks. . . ."

Patricia followed these useless pilgrimages with

deference: Where I was pointing out the garden plots, she saw a fifteen-story hospital with a school behind; the rocks? What rocks? A child's dreams, perhaps? Apartments shot up where I fought Philippe Papineau in the dust and shrubbery; this is where Robert told us about. . . . But with the landmarks gone, nothing was left of the child I wanted to describe to her, explain to her, of the child that.

"Might as well live on a construction site!"

The city like Gruyère, with unexpected holes: We didn't need wars to raze our commemorative plaques and our streets; progress alone was the equal of an American bombardment. Soon we'd have to lock up our memories . . . this curious habit of nostalgia, in a brand-new country. . . .

48

"*How many years can a bird survive?*"

"That depends on the hunters and on the bird. You know, there are gulls who've begun to live underground, on Bikini, because of – "

"Migawd! Do you think we can have a child?"

" . . . "

"I mean, allow him to live and have good reason to think he'll reach thirty?"

"We're losing feathers, my little friend."

(Nights when she behaves like that, becomes an anxious dove, I get the sudden urge to snatch out her feathers one after the other: I love you very much, passionately, deliriously, until her naked, pink body trembles with cold.

(Tonight the wind is so strong you'd think it wanted to sweep away the whole world; then she'd be dead of tuberculosis, certainly. . . .

(This nostalgia, like a favourite perfume long-lingering in the rug and the curtains, which doesn't want to let go ever again.)

49

In order to be the perfect citizen and model student, Patricia set herself the task of finding a coherent philosophical thought, daily poring over the resumés she bought from older students and condensations she found in the bookstore, telling me during our long walks about the vital rhythm and the power of a Zarathustra, whispering to me in bed, exhausted, that she was trying to reach the Nirvana of love. Her father sent her regular cheques which I used to pay the rent and keep myself in a bit of pocket money. Patricia quickly tired of the whole thing. Or perhaps it was something else: Soon, anyway, she began to take morning classes, leaving me alone in bed, and the dirty breakfast dishes on the table. I could have become a housewife and saved our ménage. But I was approaching twenty-one, and more and more I found myself thinking in terms of the collective, I talked about the masses and sacred tasks, caught up in electoral fervour.

Patricia took a lover. Except for her, I wouldn't have learned about it until spring, since:

"He's a third-year student."

"English?"

"*Of course*. He's my age and his father is very rich, they live in Westmount. . . ."

"The monstrous ghetto to the west of the Mountain where the Chateaux of the Seigneurs of Albion dominate this city which a million French slaves, with their blood. . . ."

"*Don't be ridiculous!*"

"I'm not ridiculous: You still don't understand our

romanticism; you must: For it is halfway between a baroque, absurd snarl and the endearments of a spaniel."

"*Oh, for crissake, do you have to be so pompous!*"

"That's the Versailles in me. We all have a touch of Sound and Light to us. But don't worry, you own the Chateaux. . . ."

"Okay. The show's over? I can stay?"

"Why? Isn't Sonny waiting for you?"

"You find it pretty easy to forget that we made love, *less than ten minutes ago.*"

"Do you want a coffee?"

Anything to distract us. In the tension, Patricia undid her hair which gently caressed her golden face, then fell to the first swelling of her shoulders. She shook her head to clear her forehead, something serious, something sad in her eyes which were suddenly too pale.

"He has a bachelor apartment on McGregor Street; but I'd rather live here, unless you throw me out. . . ."

"Oh, come on."

"I'm sure you'd like him, he's very nice."

"Perhaps you'd like me to invite him for dinner?"

"Later." (pause) "You know, he runs a newspaper at the university. He's very busy. President of a group to . . . how do you say '*ban the bomb*'?"

"*Antinucléaire.*"

"That's it. And then he writes a lot. He'll definitely be a great writer some day. He read me some poems he wrote for me, the start of a novel."

"Since you're paying. . . ."

(One night in Laredo I wanted to – face to face with an affable Mexican whose tequila I was buying, he listened to me more or less, repeating, 'Si, si,' at regular intervals, even if he didn't understand French, for he didn't give a damn – I tried to recapture that moment, that scene, with different dialogue. Patricia was using the same words; I changed my approach:)

"You'll like him. He's very nice."

"You. I love you."

"He runs a newspaper at the university, he's President of a *ban the bomb* group. . . ."

"You. I love you."

"And he'll be a great writer some day. He writes a lot. I saw some poems he wrote for me, the start of a novel."

"You see, Pedro, I can't win against a writer, that false being who acts more real than nature, that surgeon to whom you lend a heart and who never gives it back. The worst is, they think he has magical power. They say: He'll change life, land, love with words; like a sorcerer, with words; what idiots we are with words, Pedro, entangled, embarrassed. . . ."

Pedro laughed loudly, which pleased me very much: I was already drunk, and I had my money's worth; well-priced speeches for an attentive audience; and when the hotel bar closed. (The Englishwomen went to bed at eleven and the manager had as clients lots of Englishwomen who came on the pretext of health or tourism, to get themselves an exotic Latin male, "stuffing themselves," as the pastry-cooks would say, on an Indian specialist.) Pedro took me to the working-class district; we held each other up – I'm quite tall, and my arm around his neck gave us a certain balance – but every twenty steps, I stopped to wave my arms in the air and babble:

"Non ès turista, no, no, no, no!" (a samba tune)

Pedro had no idea whether those four words came from the baggage of Latin, Italian, or Spanish that every civilized man knows; he came back at me with the five words of English he must have learned to work on the neighbouring Texan farms:

"I friend sure work good."

To a terrace where businessmen sat in the hot night and drained iced beer and golden whisky. I stubbornly chose a table at the streetcorner, claiming that I was waiting for Patricia. Pedro simply put his nose on his folded arms and went to sleep, as if it were noon and siesta time.)

50

It's noon and siesta time. A moment ago I agreed to beat my wings at the Hillock – for the last time, no doubt. All these wounded birds, walking like wooden ducks, all these canaries of emotion. . . .

This morning Patricia received another letter from Miami asking her to care for the paternal mansion, and she insists that we go to live there; the Irish baroness is leaving (she writes) for the far-off Antilles without coming back here. She even suggests in a postscript that, if Patricia could sell it for a good price, it would be just as well to get rid of that unhappy memory of her dead husband, who had had it built the year of his death, in Albany marble and Swedish wood.

51

I'm stretched out with my feet propped up on the square sofa, I let myself go, slide, dream. Outside the milky haze of snow is still falling; all the efforts of spring and our own impatience aren't enough to melt the ice and warm the air. We sleep more and more, longer and longer, as if winter had almost used up our wakefulness. Sometimes Patricia reads verses of the Old Testament out loud.

"When you get right down to it, the Jews and the French Canadians are very similar."

I nod my peaked cap. But this analysis, a thousand times begun, a thousand times pointless, taken up generation after generation, each time leading a few adolescents to revolt and then to sleep, of course. Two hundred winters, all the same. . . .

It began around the tenth of December. It must have been 1953, which means over ten years ago: Patricia prepared dinner, bustling from cupboards to the electric kitchen then to the stainless steel sink; she told me about his books, told me that if only I'd get down to it she'd have two writer-lovers, one in each language, one in each culture, and thus all by herself she'd make a success of Canada (I think she already saw herself a celebrity and was already telling herself all the pleasures she'd have when she was old – *vieille, le soir au coin du feu, dévidant et filant* – reading in English then in French to capture the true face of her personality). I teased her, explained that New York was near-by but Paris far away, that if I decided to write (some day) it might be in English, how's that, her student and I might have the same editor in Manhattan. Patricia, beautiful, smiling over the table.

"He's called for the resignation of the Minister of Defence in his paper: I'm convinced you'd like him; I'll bring him over soon, okay?"

"You can't imagine, Pedro, how ugly I suddenly feel. Cobwebs are growing in front of my eyes."

Pedro leapt shakily to his feet, lifted his head with the eyes tight shut, said, "No, gracias, I'm not thirsty anymore," then sat down and once again tucked his nose into the fold of his elbows. The surrounding night hardly diminished the light, and children played in the street despite the hour, taking advantage of the only cool moments of all August in these niggardly deserts.

"It's just that I've got cold feet and I'm waiting day to day for the promised blow-up. You know, the day when the Americans dropped the bomb and Tokyo surrendered, I was only twelve years old; we were very proud of being so close to the U.S.A., so my friends and I played American pilot and Japanese dead for two days straight. The Japanese we killed! And they've been on my mind ever since, I think."

[The next Sunday my father took us to the country, oh not very far, for in those days Montreal was hardly a city, to celebrate the happy event with a family picnic; grandmother tucked her canvas chair under her arm and led the search for a spot without ants, where we could spread the tablecloth, napkins, the sandwiches, and the bottle of dill pickles. Well, that banquet on the grass is also on my heart; that's why, Pedro, I'm sensitive. But it doesn't show: That's art, the secret, the truth (you buy a silver knife on whose blade the worker has hammered, *Mi vida para un amor*, but you put the knife in a drawer, you never show it; mustn't advertize anything, Pedro, not anything). Patricia has this innate sense of dissimulation; I've never seen her cry, do you hear me, Pedro? Me? Cry? You crazy?]

53

Christmas came right after the first snowfall, so reassuring to children, merchants, hotel owners, skiers; Christmas came, and she spent the evening in Westmount, returned in the small hours, refused to come to bed, made speech after speech about the art of living with oneself; she paraded naked through the apartment at five in the morning, glass beads sprinkled with gold sequins at her throat, mistletoe laced at her waist, tiny bells at her ankles, her hair (which had grown) in strands to her breasts.

"I'll be your Christmas tree!"

She whirled around and crumpled.

"Come to the foot of the crèche!"

She got up planted herself in the middle of the room with her arms pointing to the carpet, the hands slightly lifted, the feet close together, making quite a faithful imitation of a decorated fir-tree.

"All I need is lights!"

I obey, winding her body with the strings of lights, leaving the red ones at the bottom, the yellow navel-high, the blue around her neck, among the glass balls. The sight of Patricia illuminated is still one of the –

"Ow-w-w!"

I had to hurry to put out the lights to end her suffering: those tiny bulbs grow intensely hot. She was motionless a moment, looking at me with the fixed fear of a wounded bird (already); I had to take off her ornaments, take her to our room, where she began – silently – to caress me, repeating endlessly, as we embraced: "Let's produce a Christ-child, today is Christmas!"

"Merry Christmas, Pedro! And long live the baby Jesus, fruit of her womb is blessed, I believed as a child; did you, Pedro? *Joder, Madona Santa!* When I was ten years old they made me – on Sundays – a ceremonial page boy. You know? Artagnon-style without the sword and fur. I wore black patent leather shoes with square buckles; and then long white silk stockings which met glossy velour breeches of dark green half-way up my leg, the Brothers, like whores, put on our lace ruffles themselves, brushed the jacket that my mother religiously prepared every Saturday night; a beautiful outfit, God, what a beautiful fantasy! Dressed in a blond wig with corkscrew curls, not girl, not boy, but holy Angel; I preceded the Chevalier of the parish (who sold life insurance through the week), carrying a brocade cushion on which rested the sword given him by the Pope or his missal bound in crocodile leather (according to the feasts of the year). Christmas Eve they put the baby Jesus on the cushion, and I carried him through the incense and the organ music to the crèche at the door of the church, a crèche is so pretty in real snow, with real straw and life-size animals, even camels and angels only slightly less than life-size; the wax baby Jesus (like a big doll) rolled a bit on the red cloth, I had to hold him like an armful of dead wood, arms at right-angles to the body. I was ten, he was one thousand nine hundred and forty-three; he bugged me with his one thousand nine hundred and thirty-three years' advantage; he bugged me the baby old-man wise-man Jesus; they still have the ceremony, I think.

That day I put an abrupt halt to my page-boy career. When I was going back into the sacristy after the ceremony, after the three slow, long Masses, I threw myself down on the stairway. I couldn't walk for a long time; here, look, the knee-cap never comes back; the Brother gave me up, replaced me with a friend who soon entered the psychiatric hospital, for someone raped him on the Epiphany. The pages never reappeared in the church, even the children from the choir made themselves scarce, the leader of the choir was sent out to the countryside, the whole thing was covered up in incense and whispers. That was one of my last Christmases as a believer. Did you get any Christmas presents, Pedro?"

54

Eaton B. gave her an otter coat, and Patricia insisted on wearing it for a candle-lit dinner behind closed drapes; but by dessert-time I was sad and couldn't laugh or reply. Patricia was vivacious, chattering about everything, modern traumas, Madeira sauce, revolutions in Latin America, children who die of hunger in over-populated China, children who find just exactly the toys they wanted under their beds on Christmas.

(I don't remember how old I was when they gave me, one New Year's, a fire-engine, with a big ladder on its back; hurled against a wall its siren wailing, the impact set off a mechanism that controlled the ladder, which unfolded in three sections; a short strip of rubber let it . . . but to really enjoy it, you had to first set a fire then extinguish it at the last moment. One day, of course, they took away my red truck. My father? Probably).

"Hey Pedro! a guy like you would have been happy there; eat, sleep, drink, that's it. Y'don't even have to be honest because nobody is; that's the system, and it's all taken into account. Just don't let yourself think, look about, doubt, play the intellectual; the bastards: the biggest bastards the earth ever knew! You know I heard some Belgians complain about the same thing, well the Belgians can put on new clothes, the pure bastards! It's us, hell is fairy tales for adults, from Little Red Riding Hood to Little Tom Thumb who always land on their feet in the end; hell is the great army of happy endings despite ogres, wolves, dense forests, hatred, deadly mushrooms, assassinations, cowardice. . . ."

But Pedro wasn't listening any more. He wandered off, singing as he went, staggering gracefully. Far off, beyond the flowering euphorbia, the sun was rising in the desert – red like the projectors in some music halls, larger than life (like an inflated sun, like an exaggeration). No light reached us yet, no heat either, but already the flies were buzzing again, circling the glasses, already sweat spotted shirts under armpits and between shoulder blades where they touched metal chair-backs; a pink and white light overcame us, like a deep, pleasant numbness. A few nights more and I would cross the border, toward the bay.

55

When the candle-lit supper was over, Patricia agreed to go outdoors, into the wind. But it was so cold that we ran from one drugstore to the next, buying coffee here and chewing gum there or a magazine; cashiers looked like the old lady at the trans-continental train stops. Trams shot sparks into the snow where ice had derailed their lines, causing a sudden lurch, a luminous rain.

Icy, wonder-struck with cold, we slid into a strange little cinema, while outside Christmas exhausted itself in a snowy powder which the wind transformed into billows at the corners of streets; we chose a dark hall while elsewhere families gathered together, usually at the paternal homestead, for involved discussion and turkey fattened with artificial hormones (since farmers are as sneaky now as yesterday), while in the kitchens cousins and aunts exchanged kisses, roasts, and recipes for leg of mutton; there were six of us in that place, only six; while in the dining rooms beer and spleen flowed, and hockey-talk with M. the priest, who has such good cigars.

There were six of us that night to look at the silk screen with its Japanese film: a story about atomic secrets in which Superboy works for the Japanese government, pro-American of course, to prevent unscrupulous spies from dominating the world.

Superboy to the rescue over their dark plans, magnificent, flying over tempests and mountains, to arrive just in time to save frightened children in a Catholic mission; at the end of the film, when all the spies were overcome, dead, or arrested, and their leader electrocuted by his own diabolical machinery, Superboy returned to the mission a little girl who had been held captive for most of the film. At the proper moment, a nun (a missionary) approached Superboy, gratefully slipped a rosary around his neck which had been blessed by Pius XII. And so, his arms crossed and his eyes turned toward heaven, Superboy rose at the speed of sound and cried: "I am an Envoy of Interstellar Space. . . . I shall return if necessary . . . when men again put your life in danger."

"I tell you, Pedro, I've been uneasy ever since Hiroshima, really uneasy."

But Pedro wasn't there any more. As he turned the corner of the plaza, he hiccuped, *"You my friend."*

"Si, Pedro, I your friend. You, the Envoy of the Stars, and me, we make a good pair of friends."

7

Patricia grumbles. We natter. She *loathes* packing, and that's all we've been doing since yesterday. It's the definitive move: in Eastview Castle we'll be living with the family servants, the old, the traditional, the Sèvres vases, the bullrushes, and the Satin-flower.

Perhaps, after all, it's the best thing that could happen to us: We'll be running a Home, a Fortune, with that feeling of real power conferred by the manipulation of money. The power of war, of sex, or death. I'll have a gilded birdcage in my room, and behind the bars I'll keep bundles of American bills. . . .

As a joke, she's made me her tutor, crowing that this way she'd have as much pleasure fooling me as seducing me. We're going to play the stock market, take risks, invest, give balls, then live in seclusion if we wish, if we so desire. Ah! to make sand-and-pebble castles at the seashore and know what privilege we have been given! And if we were to buy up the Lake in order to rebuild our childhood, clearly, passionately?

57

Passion wears out.

True, Patricia still lived on our Pacific island – third floor, end of the hall, turn left – but she went there seldom or only at the end of the day, probably in the afternoon when I wasn't present. My New Year's project had been to look for a job, and after several efforts I was employed as a salesman in a big pharmacy. Working-hours stretched dreadfully through the worst moments of the day, and four nights a week the pharmacy didn't close until two in the morning. And then I'd drive home radiant Madeleine, a pharmacy student who learned, behind the counter, to hug me tightly as soon as the customer had left. Madeleine was part of the de luxe proletariat; they had educated her to free her, she would be rich some day, and powerful, with dreams like the ones I cherished every day, but more pink and gold, with flourishes at the end of the fairy tale.

I began to think about myself, about the people I passed on the street, the steady eyes of the ones who came to buy vitamins, the deep voices of the ones who phoned in orders for French safes, as if we were a grocery store, the young girl who bought tubes of anti-acne cream every week, or the old Negro who mailed a letter to the sunny climes every Thursday, having first attached twelve cents worth of Royal stamps spat out by the automatic machine next to the soaps and toilet waters.

Madeleine and I worked together, tying up packages, preparing orders, and selling aspirin, developing a tender friendship, a workers' solidarity; time didn't stretch out quite as badly, we talked eagerly about ourselves. I wanted her to come and live on Mountain Street. She hesitated, needed coaxing. For Madeleine, it meant crossing a frontier. Accustomed to the smoke of oil refineries and the heavy smells of the East End, happy in her shirt-sleeve world, she was used to seeing the sparkle from the safety flares burning in long, polished chimneys on Notre-Dame, in the middle of blue, white, and yellow stacks, never having . . . etc. And then Patricia, etc.

But, when she did come to live with us, Patricia suddenly decided that the threesome amused her, and they were soon exchanging their baby-dolls, their skirts, their jewelry. I was the point of their barter and their kind words. In short, I was subject, and I needed a verb.

I bought a noisy motorcycle, all leather and nickel, a Harley-Davidson, heavier than a 4 cv. With Madeleine riding pillion, I'd roam the four corners of the city, like an insurance agent. White cap, padded jacket, the panache of marginal landowners. (The planet Mars, the noise, the wind, streaming eyes.)

Then, around mid-February, some unexpected encounters at student dances: a few anarchists playing at Frère Jacques, an I-chose-liberty Pole (who was consumed with remorse), literary types, dreamers, painters, a whole new society living apart from the unanimity that once was. A slightly false society, where silent girls satisfied the orators who were looking for crowds.

I quickly became part of endless discussions and useless confrontations with Europeans in exile whom I'd run across in this cultural no-man's-land.

Madeleine was in my soul, and we worked side by side (like on a honeymoon). Patricia was nothing more than a land abandoned to the first Englishman who had come along; Madeleine was that conquered country I was slowly, tenderly rediscovering.

And then love perhaps, with the new odour of;

8

Seen from the road, the Castle is the embodiment of a Prairie dream: thick towers like pregnant women, dungeons unspoiled by phoney gun-slits, three stories of cut stone, as heavy as it is pretentious; what a far cry from the wooden cabins of Swedish pioneers or the red-brick homes that the Dutch established elsewhere. The Castle has an intentionally imposing personality, it shines like all riches that have come too suddenly, too overwhelmingly, to an immigrant from Central Europe. For him, America not Israel was the promised land.

A shining horseshoe-shaped road leads to the main entrance, where four white columns support a pale balcony that would be better suited to opera than a home. But as you enter, the odour of the cedar portico catches your throat, tickles the uvula, makes you weep. And so you reach the hall with streaming eyes; the lights then become tricky and sparkling, the blond stairway whirls. The portico, in sum, opens into an emotion.

Today one must add dust to emotion; everywhere, on the furniture, white cotton dust-sheets play phantom, hiding the wood, stuffing, and leather. Eastview Castle. But it's warm and pleasant when you look beyond the park to winter, the town perhaps, while snow sifts through the windows on a breath of cold, shaped near the window by some strange milliner in thick white felt. Silence, snow, spots of sun on the pink wall. And the cook who says, "George heard crows in the park yesterday." And Patricia, who begins to flap her wings, caw, caw, running through the house, dragging me behind her until we're nothing but a pair of stubborn black birds, banging into furniture, low stools, walls, breaking our wings on glass doors, swarming up the rubber-covered stairs four at a time; then wounded, panting, short of breath, throwing ourselves dizzily on a canopied bed, glassy-eyed, beaks curved, feathers ruffled.

We used to hold council in the Expresso Bar. Madeleine went with me, but Patricia soon declared that from then on she'd look after herself, that our sessions of psychoanalysis over mugs of coffee made her vomit with boredom. Moreover, she was homesick. As for me, it wasn't hard to choose between the solid warmth of these new friendships and the scheduled love that she offered me against lost time. I let Madeleine have the trouble of consoling Patricia and the pleasure of listening to me. We used to push through the revolving door once or twice a day. The semi-opaque windows were covered with the plants, interlakes, and dreams of the rosy frost.

But once seated, warm again, our conversations were still monologues, exactly as long as the interval between two mouthfuls of beer or hot coffee. Perhaps Patricia was right. (Everyone together, barking like skinny ostriches, living in a gang, beating the air with our terrible stumps, alert eyes, half uneasy, half spiteful.)

"You see, Gauthier, when you go to the cat house, you go as one of the vanquished, ah, and you take your pleasure! When you're flush you buy yourself two girls, one hefty, one skinny, but (and this is the important point) before taking off your pants, you can't unhook your six-shooters with a virile gesture and drop them on the table. Oh, the noise of the revolver you'd put on the table!"

"You're loony."

"Loony, *my eye*! Vanquished people have always taken their revenge . . . if not, it's because they've been assimilated."

"Maybe they don't want us?"

"The English soldier, the merchant, the loyalist, even us. . . ."

"Broken backs, they've broken our backs."

L'Heureux, curled up as he spoke, analyzing the origins of our weaknesses, talking about Napoleon or Voltaire who had so many secret admirers here, but so few public ones. L'Heureux hid himself behind the mystery of his coloured glasses.

Pals, good pals, as sad as you could wish. There was Gagné, Lacombe, Bouvier, Lacroix, Jeanson Gauthier who could have just as easily been paratroopers in Algeria, pepper growers on Cayenne, declaring themselves conscientious objectors in Clermont-Ferrand, or dying, simple foot-soldiers in the loyal army of Her Very British Majesty. On short notice, we could have all joined a battalion of the Foreign Legion.

But our regiment had been decimated in 1760, and for two hundred years we hadn't taken up arms (although around 1837 there were patriots hung by the English, and then Louis Riel out there on the plains but Our arms had rusted under the bed).

"Loonies! Today! When you risk atom bombs on the head! And you dream of a battle won with two musket volleys and three strokes of the arquebus!"

An old battle, doubtless, deep bitterness, something moth-eaten.

Gauthier preened his long moustache as he talked, taking himself for a Viking; then he laughed, ripples amplifying like the waves of a shout; then he suddenly stopped short, to cough, picking up the thread of his argument. "Fools all, goddam squares, for crissake." The English came, the English won, long live the English!

Shouts of sell-out, cop-out, traitor. Madeleine soon fell asleep on my shoulder. We ordered more beer, more coffee, a sandwich occasionally, if the discussion grew interesting and stirred appetites. But the heat and the smoke grew thicker as the night wore on, and we were more and more reluctant to leave each other, to go out into the cold and wind, waiting at the doorstep to attack our warm skins, ready to shiver.

"We need blood victims, vengeance."

"What disgusts me is. . . ."

But the great trouble we took to give a name to everything! Defeat and country! These gave an identical colour to the passing days. Morning to night we looked stubbornly for the signs of servitude, the latest index of general brutishness, looking at statistics, in almanacs, horoscopes. (But we also looked for reasons to hope like a flower in the field, a new word in the language, proof that we weren't entirely vanquished.)

And then we'd go out into early-morning Montreal in groups, winding through empty avenues or along luxuriously silent Sherbrooke St. (named after an Anglo-Saxon governor who had brought us to heel), following the sidewalks like soldiers of a battalion that had been defeated so long ago so long ago, with their spent, tattered greatcoats on their backs, wearing trousers of various shades of grey, green, blue, no longer knowing if we came from the same regiment, and if it had come from Québec, or Lévis, Verchères, or Ile d'Orléans.

60

"*Do we spend this Sunday together?*"

"Aren't you seeing your student any more?"

"I like your company better, it's more – " (a gesture).

"You look disillusioned."

"He never finished his novel, he hasn't even decided to publish his poems, yes I'm disillusioned, *bored with him.* Last Sunday he made me take a train to the capital, there must have been two hundred good women to chant: *Down with Nuclear Arms!* He's on Cloud Nine, a little parliamentary activist; renting a train! *Good God!*"

By mutual agreement, Madeleine left Sundays to Patricia (who had agreed to sleep in the dining-room) and me. She used the day to go to Mass and see her parents in the centre of town, then she'd come back in the evening. Patricia no longer seemed to be affected by anything. All gold and white herself, she'd wear clinging black those Sundays as if to pose for the cover of *Esquire*), plunging me into academic discussions and then, around noon, making love to me in English. It was her way of taking a stand: *"You're completely stup: be an American and feel at ease,..."*

In those curious moments (accompanied by the record she'd put on the Philco, music to love by), I'd suddenly seize upon the whole rich strange contribution of a childhood, a particular culture, a song learned long ago (*La Tour prends garde, La Tour prends garde*), a familiar name, an evocation – each of us lives in the memory of a certain past, a certain rhythm. We were swallowed up by our words, our childhood words.

The rest of the week, Patricia wrote. She ate a lot, swam every day at the YWCA pool, only came into our room when Madeleine asked her to (the texture of four breasts stiffening under my lips). Her talk was more and more political, and we couldn't avoid misunderstandings, suspicions, a wall of nerves.

61

We had reached the age of choice. Coulombes, a dry little man with a bony face (the hardest, the most stubborn of us all) carried on his studies and his demonstrations with the egoism of a dream. He often had the happy expression of an owl which has discovered a nest of grass snakes. He roared: "You want to become a writer? Haha!"

He laughed at us, at me, saying: "You can't write a line without first choosing the metropolis you're writing for – New York or Paris?"

Of course.

62

"So you went on the road, Jack?"

Here you know there is still no road that can withstand the annual thaws! Despite the best efforts of American experts, who came to study our macadam and our cement, every spring the ground suddenly awakens, shakes itself, and the streets seize up like a wrinkled chin.

"But why were those roads to the South so precious, so appealing?" Jack Kerouac! I know you're lucky, gifted (they told me what school you attended in New York City), here you are with a mouthful of words, here you are the cream of the U.S.A.

"Still and all, you dropped us! You swapped Quebec for Los Angeles. Good old Jack! As if we weren't as fascinated by heat as you!"

(That's talent, Patricia would say: Marry America: Kiss it in your shirtsleeves!)

"Beat means beatitude?"

"Like in *beau bon bienheureux*? Brother André and Mother Marie de l'Incarnation were beat?"

No, Kerouac, for us beat means beaten, wiped out, conquered in war and commerce. You've chosen to sleep in the shadow of the White Capitol, to change the meaning of words, to become a son of Abraham Lincoln, to rub against the old Greeks of the Pentagon, under the gaze of the assassinated Kennedy. . . .

(Some days, some nights, we had a distinct feeling that everything that surrounded us was malicious, or without sense, as if time were a battered toy that could no longer make children laugh, not even the fat ones. . . .)

"Aren't you just a little bit *pink*, Jack? My elder, eh? The mulatto who managed to pass for white in the halls of the Waldorf?"

(In the smokey Expresso Bar, the jukebox was playing a Brassens that Madeleine had chosen the way you'd present an exotic flower to a naked Eskimo woman. Couples, sad or happy but above all silent, held hands, abstractedly watched us talking; Jeanson stood up every time he was talking, as if he were at a party meeting; the waitress, a pretty Swedish girl, who had only learned a few words of English in two months, had the knack of putting Jeanson into a temper over the world in general and those who made compromises in particular.)

"I know some who are dying of jealousy in this country . . . they would have snuffed out your genius, twisted it, wrung it dry. And you, Jack, you've spread it across an entire continent, our misery and your condition as a man, Saint Jack Kerouac, give us jazz, weariness, the desire to love and die exhausted on this great wheel spinning at full speed, devouring men and women, the way the Egyptians gobbled up the grasshoppers, *Amen*."

(Because we, the brave never-changing descendants of the French, obstinant peasants in Cayenne or Ville-Marie, *we* have continued to bank our money in the toes of old stockings.)

"The problem, Jack, is devaluation. Our big heavy polished coins, our sturdy peasants' coins, secretly worshipped at night by the white light of the moon, our round coins can't buy anything any more. You said, 'Keep the change, I'm taking off!' Jack, it was genius."

63

"You're forgetting to live!" said an unhappy
Madeleine who, after graduating, thought the world
would be hers. (We still hadn't learned to divide the
world between poor and rich, masters and servants.)
Or rather: God and the ghosts, or the Archangel
Gabriel smiling at Rockefeller and asking him in a loud
voice: "How can one make friends?"

64

I taught Madeleine to drive for the fun of it, and
every Saturday evening we held motorcycle races on
the ice, skimming the frozen shores of Lac Saint-Louis
in a do-si-do of yellow headlights and blue: the countryside shone in the snow, backwashes of jazz rolled out
from the Pointe Claire Hotel. Far off, very far off, students from Macdonald College jeered at us: "They're
sailing on skates, with navigation lights in the masts.
Shall we get them?"

Occasionally a ship swamped, a motorcycle put
its nose in the water.

9

"It's a death ray!"

Patricia is playing with a sharp triangle of broken mirror, holding it firmly between her thumb and index finger; she shoots a feeble ray of light on the opposite wall; the mirror almost becomes a flashlight, and its beam, reflected, fragmented, makes a round spot on the white plaster, almost perfect, its edges touched with blue-yellow.

(Her body, leaning slightly forward, well balanced on her heels, her thighs slightly opened, her breasts like ripe fruit – not pears, or grapefruit, or oranges, fruit – the sole of her foot luminescent: skin taut like the head of a drum. . . .)

The spot eclipses with dizzying speed, she flashes the light against a picture, a corner of the wall, against furniture, scans the ceiling, pierces the door: Patricia laughs, imagining the city disintegrating under her beam, the city on its knees before her.

Patricia offers herself to the world; but the whole world is indifferent and doesn't come; just her eyes, like caged squirrels. (In the National Museum in Mexico, there was a serpent of green stone which, in the same expectant pose, controlled anguish, strength, seduction.)

"Could you in my new play take the part of a mysterious wine merchant looking for a rare scent?"

"You're no longer looking for meaning in life, you want to play now?"

"I'm alive – that's what counts."

"It's an empty life, my love."

The countryside through the windows of the Castle, like so many illustrations from children's books, almanac drawings, calendar photographs below which are listed the phone numbers of general stores, and a quote from Caesar, sometimes the Bible, or Bernard Shaw.

I opened a huge jug of Chianti which I'm drinking on an empty stomach – for the joy, for the terror, for the drunkenness which comes on a white horse, I salute you Benito Fiat and Vatican, a huge jug of red wine like love, a jug to drown the fascists, the Christians, with a Roman charter, the colonists, the capitalists, the idiots, the bishops, the obscurantists, a huge jug to hide our pettiness, our shabbiness . . . . "Bring me giants!" "*Je me souviens*?" I don't want to remember anymore.

66

(That spring Montreal was nothing but stone on pavement. . . .) We undertook the simplest of tasks: Destroy a myth, replace it with another. These were the conditions of creation itself. Gauthier was writing in his big school-exercise book with its blue lines, writing with the calligraphy taught to muddle-headed children:

The St. Lawrence is the most beautiful river in the world
The St. Lawrence is the most beautiful river in the world
The St. Lawrence is the most beautiful river in the world

line after line, sentence after sentence, the same statement the St. Lawrence is the most as if to cast a spell on the world that magical the St. Lawrence formula is the most beautiful river untiringly repeated in the world pages and pages right to the Laurentians nights of setting down happy affirmations. Myth after myth.

67

The first showers.

Then the March snow, which hadn't yet melted, became coarse sugar. Children ate it as they played; for already the wind dried their lips and the ice water – in the mouth between the teeth – was pleasant, moistening the crevices, warming slowly, taking on the temperature of the palate and the tongue; swallowing it left a bitter taste in the throat and a desire for more.

68

At home without being at home.

I am at ease with you, in you, glued to your body, Patricia. I love your skin, the texture of your skin under my skimming finger, the individual odour you give your perfume. In your skin, I am well.

In my own, I'm uneasy, more and more uneasy. As if I were at home without being so. Each spring the same hopes unfulfilled. *We didn't know,* Madeleine and I. (The same way, without knowing it, a whole people, a whole city persisted in regaining the space conquered by others, the light invented by others. . . .)

The cement of the sidewalks appeared. The cold rain of April coloured the days, the accumulated snow was grey; the streets were littered with garbage, refuse, old papers that people, through lassitude (a refined form of forgetfulness), had let lie around their houses throughout the winter; it gave certain noonhours the odours and colours like the ones travellers to the Arctic say they find around Eskimo villages. . . .

That springtime I wouldn't have hesitated two seconds between the dreamed-of revolution (ogre of the drawing-room) and Patricia's bed. For in the last few weeks she scarcely came to pick up her mail; yet, despite Madeleine, everything in the house reminded me of Patricia. She hadn't taken any of her clothes; her stockings drooped over the radiators; her blouses piled up in the open drawers; her suede shoes, waiting in the hall, everything gave the impression she had just stepped out to buy a paper perhaps, cigarettes too, that she would return any moment.

Her books on the refrigerator, three dried flowers in a coloured glass with a scummy mark half-way up where the water had evaporated . . . a week? Two, I'm sure. . . .

"When you get right down to it, in this brothel they serve holy water, and you go to bed with the conqueror. I'm telling you we live in shit."

Gauthier was shouting louder and louder. Which didn't keep us from going off to our ridiculous jobs the next morning for a measly salary, which didn't keep us from trembling at the thought of losing it, work, authority . . . the virtue of obedience? Good taste even in revolt, perhaps? Or were we like those liberated slaves who couldn't get used to walking without the weight of chains (or was it ignorance? When I was ten, I remember we used to go to the mountain on Tram 29, yellow and modern and kept in the better neighbourhoods – they didn't rip up the seats, not they. However on Sunday, Tram 29 was left to families from the East End, come to admire the greenswards of Outremont. *We weren't jealous.* We were unaware even of the notion of class. For us, the rich were right: Did they leave a black Cadillac [nine seats and jump-seats] sitting in front of a huge garage, big as a suburban pavilion? They'd earned it. How could we have known what egotism . . .).

Spring settled in.

Icy, turbulent water ran off the mountain in the centre of the city in every direction; the snow melted and rushed into inadequate gutters. The children played sailor (like their ancestors), floating sticks in the pools of water multiplying at the foot of every street, in the drains and alleyways as well, when every day the sun exposed a few more centimetres of concrete, carrying out its meticulous task that would last until the full heat of summer; that blessed moment when we could wear shoes, crushing underfoot the sand that had been scattered over the ice all winter!

Blood boiled up and appetite was reborn [and the springtime Holy Thursday encouraged a local belief that a pious visit to seven churches (the seven hills of Rome? the seven capital sins? *Come on, seven, come on, seven*) and a prayer in each would shorten the time that (sinner) the visitor had to spend in Purgatory. Holy Thursday was often the first day that Montrealers went out in light coats and polished shoes, and faith knew no age. Old women made the pilgrimage – some of whom cheated, saying that seven different churches or seven times in the same church amounted to the same thing – but most of all, young girls and men, who left their districts all over the city to visit others, on foot, giving the streets a lazy holiday air.

[Short coats, powder blue, daffodil yellow, salmon pink, black suits, navy blue, collegiate blazers, a ballet under the rejuvenated sun, greetings from one sidewalk to the other, whistles, sighs, bawdy songs to attract attention. . . .

[Usually by the third or fourth visit, the boys from Immaculée would cluster the girls from Rosemont in one corner of the chapel, while those from Saint-Henri would regale those from Westmount on the landing of the fifth church, and the others, from Côte-des-Neiges or NDG, would gather in a restaurant: most of them never made it to the fifth visit, the more timid would buy a Coca-Cola in a Greek restaurant at the corner, while the others would suddenly disappear down a lane, open a garage, hide in the cars – or often behind the Presbyteries, under the huge porch.

[There, at three o'clock, which according to legend is always a time of darkened skies and cloud-veiled sun (like Veronica's veil on the face of Christ), reminding the faithful that tomorrow Jesus would once again die on the cross, Lise, Jeanne, Rose, Andrée, Louise, Michèle, and Suzanne would groan with pleasure, contentment, or misery, according to whether it was the nth, second, or first time they had received the firm thrust of a pimply student, risking a soiled Easter coat or a lost straw hat in the adventure; the students found out that if truth is hidden somewhere, it can just as well be found between two firm, unflawed thighs, ready to grip tightly.

[And it would happen that some couples, satiated, would slip into the seventh church to ease their consciences just as the lights went on in the streets, going right up to the holy table, kneeling before the sanctuary lamp – she, whispering in his ear that *those* were the dream dimensions of a genital organ worth having; he, rolling his eyes and suddenly shrinking in stature.]

Madeleine, Madeleine, we exchanged memories like merchandise in a store, making Montreal live at the level of its superstitions. The motorcycle, in spring, became a means of intoxication.

10

[Patricia is seated in a chair that is too big for her, which gives her the unusual air of a model child (*Dear child, you often say to me: "Oh! grandmother, how I love you! You are so good!" Grandmother wasn't always good, and there are many children who were as wicked as she, and who were corrected as she was. Listen to the true story of a little girl that grandmother knew in her childhood; she was stormy, she became gentle; she was gluttonous, she became sober; she was a liar, she became sincere; she was a thief, she became honest; in other words, she was wicked, she became good. Grandmother has tried to do the same. Do as she has done, my little children; it will be easy for you, for you who are not as naughty as Sophie.*

Comtesse de Ségur, née Rostopchine)

the glasses on the tip of her nose that she often refuses to wear; she has been sucking her pen, muttering as she thinks; together we are adding up the riches and debts accumulated in the fine manner of a French factory on the River Cher.]

"You never told me what you did in April that year, while – "

She quivers her finch-beak. . . .

Eastview Castle creaks everywhere like an old sailing-ship, vibrating in the spring winds which sometimes come from the semi-frozen lakes of Baffinland, sometimes from the swarming, croaking boisterous swamps of the Florida savannas, and when they meet

in the park outside the house or on the edge of the
woods behind the garden, they swirl up whirlwinds in
front of our white windows, scattering the frightened
birds which are trying to nest in the loop-holes, breaking
the icicles which – like glass stalactites lengthening
under the balconies – fall with a heavy crash; then suddenly the winds cease, suffocate no doubt, creating a
momentary silence of such intensity you think you can
hear the earth turn. . . .

*"If you ask me I don't know. She was so nice to
me and all; I loved her I suppose, really. . . ."*

Then looking me in the eyes: "You like to hurt
yourself, or is it you insist on playing the young mar-
rieds? You know, afternoon quarrels don't mean anything to me any more."

"I beat my wings, I beat my heart, but it's simple
curiosity, sister."

"He was an old man with white hair, perfumed
like a cadaver, so rich that gold dust fell from his ears
when he moved his head quickly, as for her."

"As for her?"

"I can't describe her softness; she walked in an
aura of voluptuousness; it's difficult; a living clitoris?
Between the two of them I scarcely lived, and it's perhaps because you reminded me of other realities that I
treated you so badly that day."

The university library, like a 1920's armchair,
too stuffed, too large, clinking like Aunt Ursula when
she gives a cocktail party, plush from ceiling to floor;
Gothic windows so high up that the janitor couldn't
reach the cobwebs; greenish light sifted through the
coloured glass like a meagre dust; on the wooden tables,
so heavy you could believe yourself at war, were ensconced burnished copper lamps with the switch at the
end of a long white cord; everything was so placed that
the reader could create his own velvet intimacy with
his own, individual luminous circle, separated from the
others by a wall of shadow dust, *silence, please*, in the
flat noise of leather bindings falling on tables. . . .

Patricia, at the back of the room near the library

counters (on foot, studious, intent on her work). Her professor had told me: She is finishing a thesis, you'll find her there. Thinking I'd establish camaraderie in the shadows, offering a smoke, I took her for a cigarette on the porch.

"Patricia."

"How is Madeleine?"

"Why don't you come back?"

"You're poor and the poor disgust me."

"How are you?"

"Kiss my hand." (I do as she says.) "Now bark!"

I snuffed out with my toe the cigarette she had thrown burning on the sisal carpeting, since I no longer knew what flights, what falcons, to call.

(The streets spat forth cars. I found myself walking in Montreal, hiding under the fluttering, vibrating neon signs under the dizzying posters, crying out the need for Gattuso olives, movies on Saturday night or other nights, the dry cleaners closed, and the churches open. In some districts I told myself: surely I'm on Sixth Avenue in New York, here's Fifty-second Street, what pleasure to walk in New York, you can count the stories of skyscrapers or your footsteps, or even the streets (if you forget, a sign between two traffic lights discreetly informs you), every now and then whole walls of grilled concrete, every now and then a hole, a gaping mouth the façades of buildings lacerated with tips of Puerto Rican knives, ah, New York is a great big city like its century, like it's time it's like Montreal however, which leads to Lachine, Verdun, L'Abord à Plouffe, L'Aval des Rapides, the route to the Indies. . . .

She had said with a tired smile: *I'm buying you?* With her breasts under a sweater like apples for Adam; walking along with an empty stomach, I had no trouble imagining myself *elsewhere* to escape the bargaining (in Quetzalcoatl it was the same scenario, but the dialogue was more discreet, it was the father himself who first talked money to me: He didn't want so much! but the water, si, si, that you had to buy in demijohns, coffee, the dog to feed, the daughter he loved so well, chicken on Sunday . . .).

I walked. Farther on I said to myself: How Paris
has changed; houses have grown up like kids, the
streets are bigger, the stones less grey, no more Citröen
deux-chevaux, here slept André Breton the whole night
long, no nightmares – he was a traveller – the streets of
Paris, etc. Like a poem: Rue Saint-Denis, Viger Square,
Rue des Commissaires, the whole night with a few
stops for beer, coffee, chips, until the morning, until
the light trucks appeared until the frozen pigeons until
the lazy horses; then the sleeping port only just chip-
ped from the ice; there birds white as icebergs circle
in ever-widening ellipses behind the kitchens of oil-
tankers until they're between the pale sun and me,
marking high on the wind a spot on the concrete of the
grain elevators, the spot of a furtive, uneasy shadow,
quickly devoured by the light.

(Patricia – had she thought of it? – has a name
they could have baptized a steamboat with, the first
one out. . . .)

I didn't go to work or to find the group: I hurried
into our San Francisco, there I slept heavily, exhausted,
breathless, my head full of gulls, my eyes marked with
sleeping, standing up, the verses of Pierre Loti in my
ears, and the smell of a blue whale, my son, don't you
ever want to come back, my nostrils full (with a distant, persistent hum, deadened by curtains drawn over
shut windows, the city lived twenty hours but its image
couldn't replace the dreamed-of beaches of l'Anse-aux-
Sables. I slept with clenched fists, then like a nervous
old man. But they could have wiped Montreal from
the map, levelled the mountain, I wouldn't have
known.) Madeleine waited, seated in the big leather
chair we had bought on credit.

"Did you drink a lot?"

"Who ever knows?"

"Patricia?"

"Un-hunh."

"You love her that much?"

"But no, Madeleine, it's you I – "

"Then why were you drinking?"

"Who knows?"

"Did you see Patricia, yes or no?"

"Just for a moment! She's not kept in a cage like a parrot!"

"I don't like it."

"Don't be cross with me, Madeleine, but we walked so many streets together, from the band-stand to the library yesterday, it's a little like – "

"Brother and sister?"

"No, come on. You can't understand. It'll be long and painful, that's all." I had to calm my memories into still, Prussian-blue lakes.

71

The days grew longer. Spring yielded, reluctantly of course, like a cousin at the piano; days grew warmer, the downy green of new-born leaves gave strange colours to street corners, shaming the grey shades of the walls. Madeleine was pregnant. It happened one Sunday morning. Well, so much the better.

72

When Patricia came at the end of May for her luggage (she was going home for the holidays), I found her even more beautiful than I had remembered, prettier, more at ease: and she'd learned how to apply makeup – and everything she did she did well – her curious mannerisms, mature and naïve at the same time, her softened eyes; only her laugh hadn't . . . etc. I helped her take down her bags; we were polite, friends as always, but silent because of the cab-driver who might be watching; before climbing in the taxi she turned to me: *"I believe I still love you or maybe I don't; good-bye, I don't know: au revoir!"* then without a tremor sat beside the driver, closed the door and left me in the ridiculous position of someone who's just muffed a tip. Madeleine went up again immediately. As the taxi merged with other traffic, I told myself: If you were a man, you'd run after it; then: After all it's too stupid, Patricia or someone else, good little women, the hell with them. I dragged my feet in the dry sand that coated the sidewalk since the start of construction on a brand-new building still in bags of cement and steel pylons (the black rusty chains of a crane), and went to the little cream and green kiosk, decorated with tasteless scandal-sheets, where an old Jew, scarf and mitts on as in mid-winter, disappeared under piles of papers smelling of good fresh ink and news.

A daily splashed across six columns: "Earthquake Kills 400 in Morocco"; newspaper under my arm, going back home, I was full of holy compassion for the vanished villages, for men and their condition, for the pedestrian who shouldered me as he rushed to catch an overcrowded bus that was pulling away, for myself as well, and had I been on stage instead of the sidewalk, the heroine would have begun to weep. . . .

(I was laughing at myself, sick laughter like the time Patricia talked about San Francisco, perhaps hiding from myself the fact that we're familiar with death and sorcery thanks to the radio, the papers, the news – intimately familiar – and our current conversations are full of wars, tornados, flood tides, broken dams; with every shiver of our childhood bodies, we lived the adventures of Hansel and Gretel, as real in our excited minds as Hiroshima, wolves, Auschwitz, ogres. . . .)

The same week Madeleine died (or killed herself), decapitated by a truck when she was driving alone on my motorcycle. Too heavy for her, I suppose.

Stupidly, dully, my head in my moist palms, seated at the Expresso Bar, I could only repeat one sentence (like an echo in the head), surely a sentence I had gleaned from a bad book or the movies I saw week after week (a movie, a cigarette): "Her secret will die with her in the earth . . . with her in the earth." This earth? This secret? Like the end of a film with sickly sweet music and the affected glance of the hero, in medium shot, fixed on the heroine's neck; then both of them on the screen and the hero unabashed despite all the people who are watching: with her in the earth, etc., My God, the camera begins to pull back, at full speed, as if it had had enough of this type of dialogue.

I had told them about the child. More moved than they would admit, our friends came one after the other to the Espresso. But conversation was difficult and I had no intention of helping it along. Madeleine was dead and certainly I still had to live, but how do you get rid of a body in twenty-four hours? (She had often said that she dreamed of being walled up alive, as in cloak-and-dagger novels, and one day in 1999, as they demolished the house, the Beaver Co. workmen would discover her grey skeleton between two layers of brick and plaster; papers would print her photo on page one, the Mysterious Skeleton; people would ask if it had been love or crime, and what could that house have been used for? A religious home, a bordello, the home of a minister . . . ?)

Madeleine, who loved life, died stupidly; but what terrified me even more, in that suddenly terminated adventure, was the enormous, unexpected silence; Madeleine my love couldn't add one word to what she had already said, couldn't *reply*, couldn't give birth to the son who. . . .

(That uneasy, enormous silence. In Eastview Castle, I set up an office in the south tower, where the wide stare of a stuffed owl watches me go round in circles. The owl and I are the only birds to whom Patricia would dare confide the keeping of her Chateau. From time to time, I take flight through a gun-slit, I soar, I bring back a blue flower in black moss, a white mouse by the tail, a green and brown (and yellow) frog which I lay at her feet, in homage to the one who keeps me, despite my four humps and my gnomish ways and my sadness.)

(Today I can say it; statistics don't lie; but her fortune could be evaluated just as well by the attentive, interested visits paid us by politicians and bishops. She receives them, listens patiently, gives them what they ask, and keeps perfect score on their consciences. In the evening, she invites other couples, as rich as they are handsome, to dine in our huge red-and-gold room, with the *only* crystal chandelier in all the Prairies! We're always good hosts, lively, alert. She was sixty-five yesterday. I'm 123; I've lost all my teeth one by one, blue hair has covered my head, flaccid skin has perhaps yellowed under my chin, but I manage to get around on all fours, and with dignity, even so.)

"And if hell existed, eh fellows, if hell . . . ?"

"Does your sister have a hell?"

"That's a thought! Your sister's hell interests me, because I happen to have a bit of wood to burn in it!"

"You're a bunch of fools."

We sought excuses to put off the moment when we'd have to go to the funeral home. Jeanson and Lacroix were sparring. We waited. Madeleine no longer belonged to me: Her parents had taken her back to weep over her. . . .

11

No sign set off the funeral home from its neighbours, yet it was different – a certain deliberate discretion. A vast rectangle of moulded cement faced the street, its unity scarcely disturbed by the division into floors, overpowering the ground floor of artificial stone. Black letters, somewhere between majestic and pretentious, etched into the stone.

Security, lavender, incense, and reassurance enveloped you in the vestibule. Tall, heavy lamps, flowered tapestries lined with white cotton and all-wool carpeting, diffused silence like a subtle odour, sifted by the semi-light; they had taken care to provide plenty of shadowed corners for those who wished to cry discreetly (or with ostentatious discretion).

It was only two o'clock, and we were alone (in the doorway of a hall which made you think of a whale's gullet), for people visit bodies in the evening, the way you go to the cinema after dinner.

The choice was between eight equidistant doors – four in the end wall, two on the right, two on the left – which met in a rather large corridor with a carpet the colour of Beaujolais wine. It was undoubtedly supposed to be reminiscent of a sign of love, of blood (or perhaps it was simply a colour that wore well).

Little black markers were set in the varnished wood a few inches from each door, holding white celluloid letters that spelled out the age and name:

Alain (Marie-Louise)	75 years
Charlebois (Léopold)	56 years
Deshaies (Eugène)	75 years
Guilbaut (Denyse)	26 years
Martin (Adelia)	57 years
Coulombes (Madeleine)	19 years
Roussil (Léo)	50 years
Sauvé (Alphonse)	65 years

In each salon, a half-opened coffin exposed the corpse from head to waist, the hands invariably folded around a crucifix or a rosary. And the cadavers smiled in the silence. . . .

A theatrical décor. And the little salons as empty as a church on Monday; some burst out laughing and slapped their thighs, saying: We mustn't forget to visit every body so that they won't punish us from on high – even if they don't seem bored. . . .

Madeleine's skin was waxy, and they had powdered it to hide the slightly bluish tinge. It was no longer she, Madeleine, our friend, my love.

And we were so awkward, our arms hanging at our sides, looking at the precious waxed wood, the burnished copper handles dancing with the rhythmic flames of the candles, taking the greatest care not to look too long at her face.

We didn't know what to do with our hands. Gauthier – the only believer among us – fell on his knees, his eyes lowered to the red velvet of the *prie-Dieu*, probably counting the golden nails of the coffin, cracking his knuckles nervously.

The minutes fell as heavily as sponges full of whitewash. Then I began to search for mechanical formulas, the Lord pardon them for they know not *introibo ad altare* say one one word and my soul by my fault by my fault *pater noster*, that I used to assuage pain, distracted it before, even when faced with the dentist's drill, *ave maria* but all that came to my lips were desperate cries and nursery rhymes, well Jack and Jill went up the hill *un deux trois quatre*; they had it; my soul! *ma p'tite vache a mal aux pattes* Hail Mary full of grace *tirons-la par la queue* the Lord is with thee she will get better blessed art thou amongst women in a day or two; then I found myself counting all around me *Eenie meenie minie moe, Catch a nigger by the toe* to find out which of us would be next; dizzy; sick with the stupid perfume of the carnations the chrysanthemums the roses the lilies the pansies the petunias the crocus the gladiola, tears in my eyes because I cling to this life the way a nun clings to her virginity, but squaring my shoulders for appearance's sake I went out into the hall for a cigarette. I drew slowly, deliciously, on the living odour: hot, burning tobacco. After a few moments, seeing that the others weren't following me, I ran into the street: Madeleine adieu. (It was staggering: the sound-proofed death of the funeral home had made me forget what noise we all live in. From the top of the stairs you could follow the automobiles which followed each other, fled each other, passed each other, and abruptly braked, blocked by a stubborn pedestrian, by a red light, by an unexpected jam-up; the victor's only satisfaction was to believe himself the most adroit, to lead the pack down Côte-des-Neiges, and inevitably be stopped short at a red light two streets over.)

I drew away from there, thinking: The day after tomorrow there'll be a long black hearse, a hearse as brilliant as a new telephone, rented Cadillacs, and the reunited family will follow the master of ceremonies in slow procession; trucks laden with flowers will play the tragi-comic roles. There'll be the hole dug the day before in the stony ground of Saint-Sulpice; around eleven o'clock there'll be the handful of earth, the crucifix which the priest will remove as a memento, the funeral chants, the church which I swore I would never again enter.

I walked: There'll be the final voodoo by which the women will make her death their own, will deliver her to the magical life of Christianity; they'll distribute the little photo-souvenirs where under her name, her age, her birth-place, will appear a prayer – read it for five years' indulgence – approved by Pius XII.

112

I was sick at heart and the need for air won out. I walked on, aware of nothing except that I avoided the lines on the sidewalk. My eyes saw a mixture of Patricia's smile and Madeleine's eyes, behind me I heard the cry of my son, perhaps. Soon I found myself nestling into the mountain which burgeoning summer had finally managed to seduce. As soon as the sun disappeared behind the roofs, the whispering of night moved in the trees. Every so often the guttural call of a pheasant hidden in the thicket, like a rusty pulley, made me catch my breath: I'd freeze, looking for the bird, shivering at every rustle.

(I am alone, unable to run, I draw back terrified, faster and faster as my fear grows, takes control; I run but I can't move, *powerless*; occasionally the guttural cry of a sorceress whom I recognize but cannot name makes me catch my breath: I freeze, my head between my hands, suddenly I let it fall and roll to the foot of the slope. . . .)

(In the snow this time. I'm five years old. I can't see anything in the storm, not my mother, not the cars which head for me, their lights dimmed by the thickness of the flakes; suddenly I'm up-ended; I hear the guttural cry of a man shouting himself breathless: I look for him but undoubtedly pain forces me to sleep, faint with cold. Then, suddenly, I'm terribly warm. A hospital room, a light burning in my eyes, but the sheet is white and the hand is my mother's; I drift back to sleep.)

It was stinking hot, thanks to clambering up one hillock after another and running to cling to the slopes. I crushed sunny bouquets of dandelions in the tender grass.

Shadow was spreading over the trees. By night I had finally managed not to think any more, not to think at all. I would soon reach the tourists' parapet (built during the Great Depression to keep men busy). Down below, at the foot of the cliff, you could see the city stirring, the streets lighting up, but the music from the municipal restaurant behind the trees created its own sonorous web, filling space as if Montreal had had its breath taken away and was content to murmur. Hours passed, I think, I don't know.

When I decided to move, I couldn't seem to get back to the downtown area; at every intersection I took the wrong road, dully I followed one lane after another, and suddenly came out on the Coulombes' street – after as many detours as alibis – their house was the only one still lit up.

Behind the half-drawn curtains you could see a woman (her mother?) pacing the floor, talking incessantly (the windows were half-open because of the oppressive heat, and you could even hear snatches of conversation), speaking to a man whose head was visible over the back of a dark-coloured chair.

Occasionally the new songs of green crickets overpowered the woman's monologue, and drew my attention away from those windows, as fascinating as little television screens. The air was sharp with the smell of grass, watered by automatic sprinklers. A window lit up on the second floor, adding a new rectangle of light, defining the Chinese shadow of Monique more and more clearly as she moved closer to it (I had met her a few times with Madeleine and some friends; she was hardly any younger than her sister, truly beautiful but timid, with a sort of fascinating reserve which allowed perhaps much more to be revealed than she intended to show),

Monique saw me. Probably I should have run off, or walked on with the even step of someone who has stopped to tie his laces, lighting a cigarette, casually turning my head, one hand against my face to shield the flame from the wind; she disappeared, I waited a moment, staring at the empty window; then a waxed oak door opened and she came toward me.

77

Well before dawn the air grew colder; she wanted to go back in ("I'm shivering"). At the burial, which is the only time I saw her again, Monique made no allusion either to our meeting or to the night, saying only: "Thank you for coming," in such a way that I couldn't tell if she meant thank you for coming this morning to the ceremony or: Thank you for coming, the day before yesterday, to make love in the night, in the summer.

(It can't be age that's exhausting me today; or the fact that we make love so seldom (though that certainly leads me into excessively sad moods), it must be forever circling about a well without plunging into it that upsets me. Seated at the edge, Patricia spits in the water every chance she gets. And it's the only one we have. In fact, I feel sick, not old: As soon as I stop, even for a moment, and lie down, no sooner am I stretched out on the polished tiles with my breath calm as the water, than I feel sudden pressures throughout my body, as if all my blood was in turmoil; then I begin to cough, and the racking of my legs, my thorax, the palms of my hands, and back of my neck there grow the vines, poison ivy, ferns which look like the lace leaves cut out by children in nursery classes.)

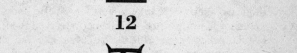

12

78

Madeleine was gone and I returned to my daily rounds. At noon, often, a greasy dust thickened the pharmacy air like morning fog, and there was no ventilation, despite the six windows, wide open. Filthy days: There was nothing to breathe but that humid mildew (clattered around the room by the electric fans) composed of soot and rain.

Then one morning I made my decision: in eight weeks at the counter, I could safely accumulate enough narcotics to fetch . . . who knows? ten, fifteen, twenty thousand dollars. Thanks to contacts at the Espresso, I could sell off the drugs in little packets. And then, the last Saturday, I could rifle the safe, just like that, etc.

Easy now, no stupidities, Madeleine would have been helpful, she who, Madeleine. . . .

"Are you crying?"

"Of course not, sir, I'm not crying: I never cry, not me."

"A tube of tooth-paste please, Colgate or Stripe, it's so pretty and how long will it take for this prescription?"

79

July was beating its drums, and M. Hoss the Manager had gone on holidays. The Good Lord was with me, I would have been ungrateful if I hadn't taken advantage of it. Every day I sold all the nirvana-producing items in the drug store. Money was building up.

Summer would be torrid in a city which, for me, had become silent and empty (storms followed the course of the rivers and we on our island were inundated daily just like a tropical country. Unusual, luxurious vegetation flourished on the Mountain, as if Mount Royal were a huge garden set down in the middle of the city to guarantee the necessary amount of chlorophyll to children, grasshoppers, to those who, despite soot, daily rounds, the exactitude of boredom, still resembled men.).

Patricia didn't write, and I had neither the humility nor the desire to be the first to send her news. Some friends stayed in Montreal until August, we began to get drunk in a different tavern every night, then to sing, laugh, break windows with friends who had nothing but the streets, eternity in hand, and security like a key-ring in their pockets.

Arm in arm, six to ten of us held each other firmly, for some grew heavy with beer like skin pouches. We always took the safest slopes, the gentlest, and set up impromptu election meetings on street corners; Gauthier on our shoulders haranging the crowd, *Aux armes citoyens!* the invader sleeps within our walls, he must be booted from the country, turn him back like cattle to the shores to the river, push him to the beaches into the sea; then, with theatrical sobs, Gauthier would recite the epic of the Acadians, the massive deportations in rudderless boats on ocean currents, Louisiana to discover, jazz born in absinthe, the Irish who – at this point in his discourse we'd begin to recite a rosary with chosen invocations and bitter curses, sometimes praying for the victims, sometimes for the hangmen. . . .

[Like tragic puppets, nerveless at the end of worn-out strings (and we didn't know who held the strings), moved in spite of ourselves, we'd sometimes walk until dawn, not wanting to leave each other, perhaps not able to, like opera Siamese, present at the disappearance of a race, and powerless.]

Finally a tepid dawn appeared, a white sun, streets to climb, others jostling with each other toward the banks of the river (I didn't tell them about my departure, nor my careful preparation of every detail of the itinerary, nor the little suitcase waiting, full of brand-new clothes), we left each other as we had any other morning, some to sleep, others to swallow two slices of toast, a cup of coffee before going back to work, a bit faded, true, but happy to have one more day to live, satisfied at having proved that fatigue will yield to friendship.

I slept the entire afternoon. Time moved on. Trams were less frequent and their wheels squealed on the rails like the complaints of adolescence, mixing with the heavy Saturday heat. That night I took the bus toward the American border as if I was off to swim at Burlington or visit a railway museum. Montreal joggled along through the back window of the bus, the millions of lights outlining its silhouette against the sombre backdrop of the Mountain began to play at glow-worm, transforming the hard, precise lines of the city into a nervous dance, staccato with pursuing fire-flies.

And with such a sum? Five years? Three perhaps? Not to do anything anymore, no work, no more trying to please, no more crawling on all fours. Rich and calm. Thirsty? Here, monsieur, at your service, monsieur; God? But that's the name given to the biggest of the bankers. In the name of the dollar, madame, you will be in my bed tonight; yesterday I was your bedside rug.

I also told myself: Rather than blowing it all, I must invest, capitalize, multiply the zeros thanks to the work of others; our dollar which art in heaven give us this day our daily percentage and forgive us our errors as we forgive those who have invested and lead us not into charity and deliver us from the poor, Amen.

Obviously this temptation of power lasted only a few days. One night, perched like a rooster at the bar of the Quality Motel in Jersey, I made speeches which embarrassed me the next day. My little generous streak had caught me by the seat of the pants. Ah, you can't escape that easily the ideals of the salaried worker! The philosophy of the weekly pay cheque, seventy-eight dollars and thirty cents, it's like a meal with garlic.

Soon I began to think that the only answer for me was to disappear completely, perfectly, like a drowned man, into the most heavily populated cities: That I would have to be swallowed up quickly in the sand of the continent, melt into the landscape like pastel-colours, vanish, become. . . .

Here! the letter S you find in U.S.A., well hidden between the other two; America, I adore you, I dress you and shod you!

("Patricia? I'll see you again some day, my little one, the hell with my city! And you, my friends, go to it, since it amuses you. I've had it, I've had boot-licking, I choose a diabolical criss-cross, I choose not to sleep any more, to be on the sharp point of awareness.")

I sought this somnambulism as hard as you could seek the other sex, a dream, alcohol. I lived in the Bronx, Toledo, Brooklyn, St. Louis, Harlem, I walked in Hoboken, I wanted to make myself accepted by the disinherited (on Twelfth Street in New York, men and women thirty years old, sixty, without shoes, without life, without pride, without nerves, without dignity slumped like bundles of laundry against condemned doors or dragging their bellies along the sidewalk for a quarter, twenty-five cents worth of rubbing alcohol; others cleaned, tended their fan-shaped feet, toes in the luke-warmth of September, others like death in the rain, dead-drunk in the rain ever since a bad turn perhaps, a father or a woman probably, a job they failed at, and they all had this instinctive fear: As soon as someone raised a hand, they rolled on the ground; afraid of a cop's hand of course, and then, the hand of the priest who wanted to be a good Samaritan – having read the New Testament – strange, villainous, disagreeable, shameful fear in the pit of the stomach; ever since Dieppe or Nagasaki probably; I was twelve, thirteen, perhaps), to become a Negro with the Negroes, a Jew among the fur merchants, Italian, Irish, wipe myself out; what a laugh: a vain effort which disguises itself as contrite humility. I followed the highways of America like long corridors between fields that were poor and green in radiant monotony; the corn (sacred plant against loss of faith) was plentiful, and in the villages they had erected cages like empty aviaries, like metalwork bee hives where they dried the ears of corn. One night, a Negro set fire. . . .

Sometimes in the morning, high up, as tranquil as the stag-beetles you see in the sand dunes at Cape Cod, grey sparrow-hawks made slow, looping circles around themselves, threw dark spots against the sun and sent the field-mice scurrying. They disdained such easy prey, happier to create unthinkable motionless movement (like saucers at the end of Japanese rods held by nimble conjurers) than to satisfy their voracious appetites.

Every time I could I'd change my name to confuse things a bit more, I become Growski, Lemay, Miller, Drinkwater, Marcovitch, Higgins, Rietpert, Pellon, Camerlain, Datko, Dutemple on the various motel and hotel registers; I bought a car as I went from east to south, then sold it and returned to my departure-point in one of those huge Greyhound buses that swallow up the tollway cement the way a calf sucks its mother, leaving behind the heavy stinking blue petrol smoke; once there, I paid a week's rent in advance at a guest-house in the suburbs; the next morning, without notice, I fled to the sea.

Months passed, and as I grew less fearful of being nabbed by the police, I became more terrorized by an uneasy vertigo which took hold of me: A little imposter looking for his parody, his next disguise. I became a child again, curious about everything, playing at the movies when I knew the area, and at eager explorer when I thought myself lost. Up with the sun, sometimes sleeping in a bed and sometimes curled up in hot sand and nettles, I spent my nights dreaming about fresh lakes and blue mountains beyond Washington, or about the birds of paradise (promised by the coloured folders at service stations) which sometimes burst into the night from gaping holes in the screens thrown up by drive-ins in the depths of fields.

Mrs. Jane Pickers received me in her home in Daytona Beach, Florida; her husband, a pilot, had been ensconced in California for three weeks.

"This will teach him that a woman is more important, by God, than the U.S. Air Force!"

(In her garden, palms spread like reassuring hands seemed to create wind just as the sea seemed to calm it. Mrs. Jane Pickers was upright on the squares of cement despite a lot of whisky, her legs just slightly apart to ensure balance.)

There were Jane Pickers in Dallas, in Port Hope, in Baton-Rouge, in Toledo, so what?

82

We're not going to play any more, Patricia. The snow melts. We won't play any more. At least, not for a long time. The games are over; here we are, like adults at the breakfast table, looking in each other's eyes (blue, green), over cups of instant coffee.

"We haven't, perhaps."

"Something else bothers me; I think I'm really bored here, you. . . ."

"Thief!"

"Blond hair the colour of a woman of the north, a little band-stand for German opera, American breasts, aggressive cruisers, freckles artfully spread. . . ."

"Through with literature?"

"*Never*; but all that (sweeping gesture that covers her from head to foot) – anyway, has never been entirely mine, it's – "

"*As if I had been paying you to make love?*"

"If you like; but I'm not at ease here; and your countryside – "

"Now you're being ridiculous; *sugar, please.*"

"Patricia." (All that is unhealthy. Those feathers that cover us as if we were flowery birds.)

("When the winters are really bad they die by the thousands; in the spring, when the sap's running, when the sun makes the water run, the downy bodies rot to the bones; later, much later, summer and the migratory flocks allow us to forget.")

13

83

The Castle, which had been as static as a Christmas card, became once again a wealthy bustling house. And the only reminder of winter is those puddles of water which are everywhere and soak the yellowed lawns of the boulevard.

Tomorrow: Summer, people. Things are sorting themselves out.

I explained everything to Patricia; she didn't understand, but really, *it doesn't matter.* There are millions of us who understand, well nearly. Yesterday morning in the *Free Citizen Gazette,* a four-column spread with photographs, a story wired from Montreal by Canadian Press:

**UN VEILLEUR
DE NUIT TUE**

Avant-hier soir, samedi, le Front de Libération québécois a fait sa première victime: Vincent O'Neil, veilleur de nuit au centre de recrutement de l'armée, rue Sherbrooke.

Les autorités du Québec ont annoncé une récompense de $50,000 à quiconque pourra donner des renseignements menant à la capture des membres de ce réseau terroriste.

On sait que le FLQ, depuis la destruction du monument Wolfe dans les plaines d'Abraham, n'a cessé de harceler les forces armées, la R.C.M.P., et que les membres ont juré qu'ils détruiraient le colonialisme et ses symboles.

**FLQ'S TERRORISTS
BLAMED FOR BOMB
DEATH**

(CP) The terrorist Front de Libération québécois today bears the brand of assassin in the wake of Saturday's explosion-killing of a National Defence furnaceman, who was due to retire next month.

While Quebec officials hesitated to blame the murder on the FLQ directly, it became known that Premier Lesage has them under constant surveillance.

The victim of Saturday's killing was William Vincent O'Neil, 65, a veteran of two wars, who has been employed at the Army Recruiting Centre on Sherbrooke St. W.

On ne sait, pour l'instant, si le FLQ est d'obédience marxiste. Le gouvernement s'inquiète de ce que les tracts distribués ressemblent à la propagande castriste.

Vincent O'Neil, âgé de soixante-cinq ans, prenait sa retraite le mois prochain. . . .

Among the measures aimed at eliminating terrorist activity in Quebec will be legislation placing tighter control on the sale of dynamite, the Deputy Attorney-General said Sunday night. Government buildings also have been under tighter watch in recent weeks.

Since the destruction of the Wolfe Column on the Plains of Abraham in Quebec City, FLQ terrorists, who claim to be Marxists fighting for freedom, remain an organization of mystery.

Who are the members of the FLQ? How many are there?

The FLQ pledged to destroy all symbols and colonial institutions, in particular the R.C.M.P. and Armed Forces by systematic sabotage. The search goes on, police said.

84

Time to pack a bag, to leave, probably to break my wings.

To destroy the birdcage, *to choose.*

Eenie, meenie, minie, moe, Catch a nigger by the toe, If he hollers let him go, Eeenie, meenie, minie, moe. To choose, with clenched fists.

(Hatred has come, like a season. Spring has come, like a slap; nobody can fight the wind, the seasons, white light, snow tousled by gusts of wind.)

(I won't do you any harm, if you stay silent, Patricia.

(Anyway it wouldn't do you any good to struggle or to cry out, or to recall our love that was. The knife will stay on the table. No trace of blood on the carpet.

(Your soft, vibrant body will hardly quiver, your breath will hardly. . . .)